FOUR OF FOOLS

Other novels by Evelin Sullivan:

The Dead Magician
The Correspondence
Games of the Blind

FOUR
OF
FOOLS

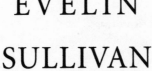

EVELIN
SULLIVAN

FROMM INTERNATIONAL
PUBLISHING CORPORATION
NEW YORK

Published in 1995 by Fromm International Publishing Corporation, 560 Lexington Avenue, New York, NY 10022.

Manufactured in the United States of America

Designed by C. Linda Dingler

Printed on acid-free, recycled paper

First U.S. Edition 1995

Library of Congress Cataloging-in-Publication Data
Sullivan, Evelin E., 1947–
    Four of fools / by Evelin Sullivan. — 1st U.S. ed.
      p.   cm.
    ISBN 0-88064-166-5 (hc : acid-free) : $19.95
  PS3569.U3467F68   1995
  813'.54—dc20   94-45389
                                                       CIP

To Mike

FOUR OF FOOLS

I HONESTLY BELIEVE THAT ON THE DAY MY WIFE AND
I and our best friend left New York for Italy, she intended to
kill a man. Or is *intended* too strong a word for what was only
the germ of a wish? What do you call phantom thoughts that
flicker in the brain as the image of a corpse on a marble
slab—no visible wounds, but the scene infused with the special dread of knowing yourself somehow responsible for the
monstrous stillness of that naked man?

I have at any rate no reason to doubt that death was on
her mind when on our first day in Rome the three of us wandered through a museum of Etruscan artifacts. I forget whose
idea the museum was. Not mine. I would have been happy
enough spending the afternoon strolling down streets and
haphazardly stumbling across the odd monument or ruin.
But "When in Rome, do as the tourists," quipped Vida (as in
"mi Vida, te amo"), and the guidebook she bought was of the
"while at the Villa Borghese, don't forget to . . ." sort. Which

suggests that the Etruscans were her idea. Then again, Jim's eclectic interests and a morbid streak that I hadn't yet learned to appreciate may have been responsible for our finding ourselves in the presence of trinkets and utensils, photos of excavations, and an ambitious mock-up of a tomb—all connected with the elaborate necropolises constructed by people who strove mightily to believe in the afterlife as more of the same. Our friend studied the photos of funeral chambers and of the colorful frescoes at their entrances, while Vida briefly but conscientiously looked at every vase and plate on display in room after room crammed with glass cases. I commented on the startling elegance of this or that reddish-brown-on-black figure depicted on the pottery, but my wife's aesthetic sense was not in operation; she nodded and moved on. I lagged behind but finally caught up with her standing before a massive sarcophagus depicting a man and a woman lying on their sides, propped up on their elbows. I was tired from the unaccustomed rigors of tourist life and sat down on a bench. I looked at Vida—a more arresting sight than the uncomplicated depiction in stone of two not extraordinarily handsome people who had been dead these two thousand years. I watched her—the observer observed—standing with the athlete's broad stance, her head pensively tilted to the side as if pulled over by the massive braid of flaxen hair that would have looked dull on any other woman, pale blue shirt, jeans, low boots, a mountain parka under one arm, manly in height and slenderness, Artemis the huntress in modern outdoor garb.

How little I knew her! So very little that my ignorance strikes me as miraculous now. (Anyone who, after I'm through telling my story, wishes to argue that it takes more than ignorance, it takes a deliberate reluctance and cultivated opaqueness, for a man to know as little about his wife of five years as I did then, will find me agreeing. But I also challenge any husband to produce a wife as committed to keeping secrets as my Vida.) There I sat, irritated at her earlier perfunctory treatment of superior art and sudden interest in those two mediocre effigies of polished red marble: man and wife looking at eternity with a sightless gaze and frozen half-smile that suggested to me either vacuousness or a sculptor unable to breathe any semblance of life into his creations. And there stood Vida, seeing what in those awkward figures? a state of grace? happiness? love?

But I'm casting myself as more ignorant than I was. On some level I must have known full well that those figures had meaning for her, and I must have refused to turn my mind in the direction of the what and why of that meaning. How else can I explain the vividness with which the scene remains in my mind? And my sudden thought that Vida was lost in a dream?

Then Jim joined us and said: "Till death do them part—except it doesn't seem to have." Vida nodded slowly, unwilling to leave her dream. I stood up and observed that two figures on the same sarcophagus didn't necessarily mean the couple had died together. It may have been not uncommon to commission both figures at the same time; maybe one got a discount.

"Still, it's a charming thought, isn't it?" said Jim, looking to Vida for approval. She shrugged and resolutely turned away from the sarcophagus.

We followed Jim to a discovery he had made: a full-scale reproduction of a salacious fresco found at the entrance to one of the tombs according to the description. One naked man bent over, about to be buggered by another, equally naked one, sporting a heroic phallus. "One can tell these people believed in a hereafter. Earthly delights of all kinds," Jim said.

"And sizes," commented Vida, her old wry self.

But at dinner she talked about the figures on Etruscan sarcophagi, which according to the brochure she had leafed through were famous for their haunting smiles. Jim of the cosmopolitan palate had ordered wild rabbit, and to my surprise, Vida, who had never before shown a hankering for hunted food, had followed him, placing her order with a defiant expression. Not addressing either of us, but studying the dish before her, she said, "I don't think *haunting* is the right word. To me they look . . ."

She seemed uninterested in completing the sentence, and I did it for her: "Serene?"

She ignored my contribution. "So at ease," she said to her rabbit in sauce. "Unafraid, and like they belonged together—not like two people just accidentally in the same place."

I was about to point out that that impression was due to the facial similarity of the couple, which conceivably had more to do with an artist able to carve only one type of face than with two people in a happy marriage, but Jim found the more winsome thing to say: "Maybe they really did believe that they'd still be together on the other side."

To which Vida replied (to his face, not to the murdered hare before her): "They couldn't possibly have been that stupid."

✳

Back at the hotel I took a shower and got ready for bed. When I came out of the bathroom, Vida was sitting on the bed, studying her brochure on the Etruscans.

I had been thinking about the exhibits, and I said, "It really is amazing how much of the gross national product went into cults of the dead in these ancient civilizations. And the Etruscans are a relatively mild case. Think of Egypt—millions of metric tons of stone piled up, slaves wasted by the tens of thousands, gold sarcophagi. And all for what? For the sake of a few dried-up corpses."

Vida, lifting her eyes briefly from the brochure, said, "They didn't think of it in those terms."

"No, of course not. But considering it abstractly—suppose you'd just landed from Mars—it does sound bizarre to devote that much in effort and resources on something so patently futile. Of course a Martian might say the same thing about the great cathedrals or anything else having to do with blind faith."

I should have known from Vida's terse comment that my theoretical rumination had planted the germ of an argument. But I also had every right to expect her to concur: in all the years I had known her, she had never shown the slightest interest in the hereafter. So I was startled when without taking her eyes from her reading matter she asked, "Does it ever amaze you how little imagination you have?"

I said, "What do you mean?"

She began flipping the pages rapidly, using the activity as an excuse for not looking at me. "It's a simple question."

"You mean does it amaze me that I don't have a lurid imagination? I don't understand. Am I suddenly supposed to be enthralled by a system of beliefs that holds that the dear

5

departed continue merrily in the beyond provided you gut them and pull their brains out through their noses?"

She finally gave up on pretending to be interested in the brochure and tossed it aside. "Of course you don't understand. And, no, you're not supposed to be enthralled by anything. But some day you just may find that a lurid imagination is the only thing that has the slightest chance of doing justice to life."

"To whose life? Mine? Yours? When last I looked, neither of us was acting particularly luridly."

"Everybody's."

The single word, uttered with precision and emphasis, squelched the incipient argument. I was stunned by its ring of bitterness and said nothing as Vida got off the bed, brushed past me into the bathroom and closed the door firmly. A short while later, the sound of running water told me she was taking a shower. I went to bed intending to stay awake until she came out of the bathroom and to ask her why she was in such a rotten mood at the beginning of a trip that hadn't been my idea in the first place; the pseudo-vacation she had billed it as would have a better chance of success if she didn't go out of her way to be disagreeable. But I fell asleep before she had finished her shower.

✳

Why was Etruscan funeral art the highlight of our first day in Italy? Random chance according to one school of thought. An emblematic hint of things to come according to another. By that other view, a pattern had been started at one of the four corners of the universe and matching pieces were beginning to pop up with ever greater frequency. I suppose I've been converted to view number two because now that the entire garish picture is complete, I see the individual elements everywhere. I see one of them a year before our Italian excursion: Jim Quarrel saving my life on a winter afternoon. Another one is certainly to be found much earlier, in Vida's weak and ineffectual father walking into the path of a locomotive. And yet another one even earlier, in slim, prepubescent Vida being loved by a satyr in a shaded grove. Not that I was ever given an honest rendition of either of those traumatic childhood events by my wife. I had to hear them described by a third party to get any idea of the damage that had been done to her. Which explains at least in part my perfunctory compassion when five or six years earlier she had told me coolly, clinically, that her father had committed suicide when she was fourteen, and that she had routinely been sexually molested by her father's adviser and friend between the ages of ten and twelve. What was easier than to respect her obvious wish not to have wounds reopened and to dispense with a more detailed account of these horrors?

But now I'm putting all the blame on her, when I was equally to blame for my ignorance, that willful blindness that made me stumble along a precipice and never deduce from the updraft at its edge the drop onto jagged rocks. Whoever thinks he has the slightest idea about the human heart is in as precarious a position as the man who thinks he understands the workings of the cosmos.

✳

We spent one more day in Rome, since Vida's research project, the remarkable Geoffrey Fry, was at a conference in Tel Aviv and was not able to welcome us at Frascati until his return. Then we took the Metro and the bus to the town, picturesquely situated on a hill and surrounded by woods and vineyards. We arrived around 11 A.M. and took a cab down narrow roads flanked by new and old buildings, many a salmon pink that reminded me of Etruscan pottery, to the Institute of Nuclear Physics. There, at the gate, we were eyed warily by the guards, who seemed unsure whether to focus their distrust on the young male with the crew cut, beard and earring (Jim), or the middle-aged man with the dissipated Irish face and a mane of black hair (me), or the tall woman in jeans and a faded parka.

Jim, who knew a smattering of Italian, showed them the letter Geoffrey Fry had sent Vida, inviting her by all means to come and pick his brains for the book she intended to write. He pointed to Fry's name at the bottom of the letter and told them Vida had talked to him on the *telefono* the night before and *il professore* expected all of us. They studied the letter skeptically, but one of them picked up the phone, talked to someone, and five minutes later we were greeted by Fry, who apologized for the suspicious reception, explaining that visitors were usually met at the airport by a driver known to the guards. Fry was a thin, balding man with a short mustache and alert eyes that darted over us, alighting on Vida, on me, on Jim, again on Vida, as she introduced me and Jim Quarrel. He shook Jim's hand and said, "You have an interesting name."

Jim said, "But inappropriate. I'm as peace-loving as can be."

Fry laughed and said, "A wonderful quality." He did not

comment on the fact that my last name was not the same as my wife's, but I had no doubt that he made a note of it when he shook my hand, saying cordially, "Is that the trace of a Boston accent I detect, John?"

I said, Yes, even though I hadn't set foot in Boston these ten years.

Through the flurry of activity that followed—Fry explaining the procedure for getting Vida a pass for the Institute, asking her for her passport to show it to the guards and talking to them in rapid Italian, Jim translating for us what was going on, or his guess of what was going on—I could nevertheless tell that Vida was nervous in the presence of the great man: she twice made the same joke about the guards apparently suspecting us of being international terrorists and got flustered looking for her passport, dropped it, bumped heads with Jim in picking it up, acted as if she hadn't bumped heads with Jim. Fry noticed everything but graciously acted as if he didn't, clearly not wanting to make her even more nervous.

The plan was for Vida to spend many hours with him in the next four weeks since he would be the cornerstone of her book on the scientific mind's processing of reality, or, as I insisted, "reality," an ambitious step following her Master's thesis in an interdisciplinary field melding history, sociology and science. Her subject had been one Sir Isaac Lintot, a "Natural Philosopher" in Charles II's Royal Academy. Lintot's claim of having created "all manner of insects, worms & deathwatch beetles from the sole elements of putrescence and foetid air" made him one of the more amusing members of the Academy as well as a minor monkey wrench in the development of the scientific method.

The admission procedure completed, Fry took us to his

car, a black Mercedes, telling us about the apartment he had arranged for us at a villa kept by the Institute for visitors. It was a brisk ten minutes' walk from the Institute. "You'll find that everything in Frascati is a brisk ten minutes' walk from everywhere else," he said.

Fry drove too fast for my sense of what was safe on the narrow cobbled roads. "The drivers in this country are very good," he said as if in response to my worry. "But they do make mistakes, so it's a good thing to be alert when you're out and about." He passed within inches a teenage boy walking next to a wall.

"He didn't seem too alert," Vida commented. If she was still nervous, she no longer showed it.

"He didn't have to be," Fry said. "I don't make mistakes."

Vida was sitting next to him; Jim and I were in the backseat. Without taking her eyes off the road, she said, "Must be a blessing to know that."

Fry took a quick look at her. "A slice of wry?" he asked. Then he swung into a driveway appearing as a gap in a wall and came to a sudden stop before an iron gate. He told us to stay in the car, got out, took a handful of keys out of his coat pocket and inserted one of them into a box mounted in the wall. The electric gate swung open with a low hum. Fry drove a short jaunt up the driveway to a cubic, salmon-pink two-story house. "There are three apartments—two on the bottom, one on top. I got you the one on top. It's bigger and has a view. No other visitors are expected for the next few weeks, so you'll have the whole villa to yourselves."

We thanked him and followed him up the tiled stairs to a pleasant living room with a view of the lowland and (Fry told us) of Rome on a clear day. In a corner was a small kitchen, and down a short corridor were two bedrooms and a bath-room. "Not palatial but, I hope, adequate," Fry said. Then he drew us a map to the nearest supermarket, "about ten min-utes' walk from the villa," and offered to pick us up at eight for dinner, so he could get to know us. We gladly accepted, and he left us to get settled in.

We did so in short order. Jim took the smaller, one-bed bedroom, Vida and I the larger, two-bed one. We lugged toi-letries into the bathroom, hung up things in wardrobes and put them in drawers, and agreed that the accommodations were splendid, and Fry incredibly nice.

Fry picked us up at eight o'clock sharp and drove us to a minuscule restaurant with no more than four or five tables, which had as its two waiters the portly owner and his ten-year-old son. There he treated us to a six-course dinner accompanied by three different wines. He explained the items on the menu and, when we had ordered, told us an amusing anecdote from his first month in Frascati. He had given a ride to a hiker, who, based on a few colloquial Italian phrases Fry had ventured, had assumed he spoke Italian and had talked at him for a solid hour about something Fry had guessed to be either pig breeding or Mayan architecture, but that had finally turned out to be a type of nineteenth-centu-ry earthenware the man collected.

But Fry didn't monopolize the conversation. He asked us about our two days in Rome, sights seen, things done, what our plans were in Frascati, what Jim did when he wasn't trav-eling with friends. He was inquisitive and attentive when

Jim—by some association I forget—told him his story of a stint in the navy during which he had participated in ethically questionable experiments on hypothermia. In one study, investigating the effect of alcohol consumption on loss of body heat, Jim, thinking himself a lucky son-of-a-bitch to have been accepted for a cushy special assignment, had sat in a tank of fifty-degree water, sipping vodka. After four or five shots, he had been too drunk to care that he was dying under the nose of the equally drunk experimenter while a battery of sensors dutifully monitored his falling body temperature and the approach of his circulatory system's collapse. Only the chance appearance of another experimenter had saved him.

I'd heard the story several times and had never found it more than mildly amusing, and I was surprised to see Fry laughing out loud.

My own life, as I told our host when he asked, was short on amusing incidents—unless two years in the Peace Corps in darkest Africa could be considered amusing, or two wasted years of graduate school in sociology, or writing a book that in all probability no one would want to publish.

"What's your book on?" Fry asked, and I gave him a thumbnail sketch of Joshua Anders, my remarkable great-uncle on my father's side of the family—South American explorer, photographer, inventor.

"But you're a professor of history, aren't you?" Fry asked.

I wondered what other salient facts Vida had mentioned in her letters to him. Ex-professor, I said; the result of not getting tenure despite a not insubstantial list of publications. The usual academic internecine warfare over whose golden boy would get the plum, I added.

"I'm sorry to hear that," said Fry. "The best revenge is to publish your book and have it be hugely successful." Then tactfully changing the subject, he wanted to know how we had met our friend Jim.

I told him the story of Jim saving my life. It had, almost a year after the fact, become a well-honed tale, told with just the right amount of sardonic wit leveled at my undynamic response to the danger to life and limb and at Jim's take-charge approach (and with no mention of my terror at the boozy reek and enraged eyes of my assailant). Jim, as usual, protested that he hadn't saved my life—at most he'd kept me from getting a cut or two from the rusty linoleum knife in the hand of that mental case. "Yes, a cut or two from ear to ear," I said. "Inconvenient as hell."

We all laughed, but the feeling I got was that Fry was not satisfied with the story. He was on the verge of asking me a question. "Why didn't you . . ." he began, but quickly shook his head as if a more important thought had driven out what he had meant to say, and he alerted the owner's son to the fact that we needed more wine. For some reason his behavior struck me as exceedingly odd. I should add that to me everything about Fry seemed odd on that evening, a thing I became half-conscious of only with that unasked question. I didn't analyze the feeling then, but when I later recollected the dinner, I seemed to remember the impression flitting in and out of some peripheral consciousness that Fry's charming attentiveness and interest were hiding something else, and that our answers to his questions were either the wrong ones or the right ones to a wrong interpretation of what it was he was asking. Quite possibly my impression of something strange, disguised, murky, had more to do with the

13

serious case of flu I came down with on the next day than with a preternatural awareness of things to come or of danger. I know that Geoffrey Fry would disagree with me and would claim that danger was precisely what I sensed. And he would probably be right. For we were, of course, all four of us, in mortal danger from the moment we met.

How Vida had decided on the unusual topic of her book was Fry's next question, and I draw a blank in trying to remember what she told him. She probably mentioned a lifelong interest in science from a layman's point of view—her father had been a scientist—coupled with an equally strong interest in the humanities. Fry must have asked her about her father because I do remember her telling him that he had died of an embolism when she was fourteen, an understandable lie, since who could blame her if on that pleasant evening she didn't want to call up the specter of a man unhappy enough to have wanted to be cut into pieces by a two-hundred-ton locomotive?

They also talked about her last name. Fry wondered whether she was related to Samuel Morse, of Morse-code fame. Not as far as she knew, she said. And was Vida short for anything, he asked, or was it simply *life* in Spanish? She told him it was short for Davida, the feminine form of David. Fry said he had always been interested in the etymology of names. He found that far from being random, names frequently related in meaningful ways to people's personalities and lives. They also entered into his current research project. He seemed about to change the subject, but I asked him what his project was. He laughed at a private joke and refilled his and my glass. Then he said that one of the great benefits of being famous and old (he was in fact fifty-four) was that he

14

could finally do all the crazy things he'd been wanting to do for the past twenty years without the risk of being fired. The Institute paid him handsomely for the privilege of having him, even if they said behind his back that poor Geoffrey had lost his marbles.

Vida had told me about Fry the prodigy, and I had read the article in which she had "discovered" him and which had given her the idea to contact him: a B.A. in physics at seventeen; a Ph.D. in high-energy physics at twenty; predictor of an elementary particle resonance subsequently experimentally verified; inventor of an elegant topological theory that was still the closest thing to a unified field theory; virtual shoo-in for the Nobel prize one of these years. Even past accomplishments aside, "poor Geoffrey" did not look to me like someone missing any of his marbles.

"What crazy things are you working on?" asked Vida. "I've read your article on meaningful coincidence, but I wouldn't say the idea is crazy."

Fry laughed again. Then, studying a fold in the white tablecloth, he pondered his answer as if he were trying it out, discarding some parts, refining others. I was about to tell him that he didn't have to justify himself to us when he looked directly at Vida and asked, "Are you sure you want to know?"

Which made Vida lower her eyes and reach quickly for her glass of wine. I rapidly thought that he meant to seduce her, that she would be willing, and that their affair would end our marriage. Then I thought that I was having an attack of galloping paranoia.

Vida drank a few sips and observed sensibly that she hardly had a choice in the matter—if she was going to use him in

15

her book, she had better know what the scientific mind of her prize subject was up to.

"True," said Fry. "But you'll have to promise me that you'll keep an open mind. And the same goes for Porthos and Aramis," he added, looking at Jim and me.

"Who?" asked Jim. Then he remembered, "Oh, the Three Musketeers."

"Athos being the third," Fry agreed.

"Or were they Groucho, Chico and Harpo?" I asked and we all laughed.

Then Fry sketched for us his theory of meaningful coincidences, or rather his extension of an old theory, developed by the Austrian biologist Paul Kammerer and published in 1919. Kammerer had postulated, and attempted to prove through a wealth of recorded observations, that coincidences are not random events but the manifestation of an "acausal force" that acts selectively on the universe to generate similar configurations in space and time. Examples of the phenomenon were everywhere: the same esoteric word unrelatedly cropping up several times on the same day; someone moving from an apartment building where the manager was an ex-actress to one where the owner was an ex-actor, to one where his next-door neighbor was an aspiring actress; a man marrying three women in the course of his life, all of whom had years earlier worked for insurance companies; a streak of good or bad luck. Kammerer referred to a "correlation by affinity," which appeared in coincidences of this type and in popular sayings like "when it rains, it pours" or "speak of the devil" and in the notion that things always come in threes. The man struck many as a crackpot, Fry conceded, and his professional reputation was severely damaged by evidence that a land-dwelling midwife toad, his prime specimen for proving the existence of a non-Darwinian process of evolution, had been tampered with. The charge was that Kammerer had used india ink to give a dead specimen, bred and raised in an aquatic environment, a semblance of the "nuptial pads" with which its aquatic cousins held on to the female during copulation. But no less a figure than Einstein was interested in Kammerer's idea of "laws of seriality," and C. G. Jung had dabbled with it in his own essay on what he called "synchronicity."

"But isn't it true that millions of things are constantly happening and we just become aware of the few that are coincidences?" Jim interrupted.

"That's always been the argument of skeptics. Kammerer's answer to it is that, on the contrary, there are far more meaningful coincidences than we ever recognize. Let me give you an innocent example concerning the three of you. The day I got Vida's first letter, I found on a lawn at the Institute a copy of a page with the Morse code on it. Interesting coincidence, I thought, then I saw that on the back of the sheet, someone had written in Italian, 'Giovanni, I couldn't find the James book; can you help me?' So there was not only the correlation between Vida's name and the Morse code but that between the planned book she was telling me about in her letter and this message about a book. The other connection, that of Giovanni and James—John and Jim—occurred to me only today after I met you. The thing is, I ordinarily would have declined a request to allow myself to be shadowed by someone. I would have considered Vida's offer an avoidable disruption of my life and would have politely answered no. But I was intrigued by the coincidences I saw. So you owe your presence here and now to a coincidental universe."

Jim was not convinced. "But you must have found other pieces of paper in the past with writing on them, and if they weren't connected with anything, you just threw them away."

I was puzzled that Vida, knowing more about Fry's subject than Jim or I since she was the only one who had read Fry's article on coincidence, was staying out of the discussion.

"Or were they connected with something and I didn't recognize the connection?" Fry countered Jim's argument.

Vida finally broke her silence. "But isn't it highly unlikely that somewhere in the universe something kept track of the fact that my name is Morse and that I wrote you a letter, and that whatever that 'force' is made someone copy a page with the Morse code from a book and then use the back of that page to write a message concerning a book and a John and a Jim, and then made him lose the page where you would find it just after you had gotten my letter—and all that just to generate coincidences?"

"Or maybe it wasn't even the same guy who copied the page; maybe he found the page in a pile of scratch paper," Jim added. "At any rate, you'd have to assume that this acausal force makes all sorts of people do all sorts of unrelated things at different times, always with the aim to make these things meet up coincidentally. So there still is cause and effect, only in a weird way: something caused Vida's name and the Morse code to show up at the same time, and the effect is that we are here."

Fry smiled. "That's a good description of the problems you face when trying to dissect the process. But you can recognize a process in action without necessarily understanding it. People watched falling objects for tens of thousands of years and had no idea about gravity as a distortion of space-time."

Jim was not about to give up. "Yes, but they knew that every time they threw someone off a cliff, he fell down."

"Cause and effect," Vida agreed. "Even if they didn't know why, they knew that the same thing would always happen. If they let go of something, it would always fall. Whereas there is no way you can make a coincidence. Not without violating the meaning of coincidence."

I felt a dull ache behind my eyes and it seemed silly to me that Vida and Jim were arguing about something they knew next to nothing about, and with someone who was probably smarter than the two of them put together. Fry didn't seem to mind. His eyes moved from one to the other with a lively interest. "That remains to be seen," he said. "That very much remains to be seen. But at any rate classical causality is a dull concept when all is said, and in my opinion the universe becomes infinitely more interesting if causality is complemented by coincidence."

We had finished dinner some time ago and were lingering over cappuccino. Fry checked his watch. "I want to show you something," he said. "Unless you're too tired."

Vida and Jim protested that they weren't in the least tired—not after all that excellent food and wine, and interesting conversation. I was tired and my head ached, I assumed because of the wine, but didn't say anything.

"Onward then," Fry said, and called over the owner to settle the bill.

When we got into the car, Fry said, "What I have in mind is one of the local peculiarities. This is the ideal night for seeing it by the light of the silvery moon."

We left town in a matter of minutes and drove, too fast I felt, along a country road toward the gibbous, more buttercup-yellow than silvery, moon. "What I'll show you, surprisingly, hasn't appeared on any tourist map so far," Fry told us after a while. "When I first found the place five years ago, I thought that the lurid story connected with it should have made it a prime candidate for guided tours, but maybe it's too far off the beaten track."

"What's the lurid story?" asked Vida.

"Oh no," Fry laughed. "First you have to see the sight with a gasp and a shiver."

I don't think any of us gasped when a short while later he turned onto a dirt road and, after a bumpy quarter mile or so, a tower, gray and massive in the moonlight, appeared over the trees. But I know I shivered when I got out of the car— whether because of the damp cold, or my incipient flu, or an attack of prescience, I don't know.

Fry had parked the car under a stand of trees and we caught glimpses of the tower as we made our way through the trees in the dark.

"It's amazing. How old is it?" Jim asked.

"Not very by local standards. Early eighteenth century. It was built by a mad duke who hanged himself in it."

"Is that the lurid story?" Vida asked.

"Is there a ghost?" Jim jumped ahead.

"No and no," said Fry. "The lurid story is grimmer, and there should be a ghost connected with it, but there isn't."

Jim was right. We stepped out of the trees onto an amazing sight: the tower was square, not very tall—maybe the equivalent of a modern seven-story building, but forceful in its unadorned primitiveness. It had a door, heavy and studded with iron, and several small windows, boarded up from the inside, at various heights.

I was astonished when Fry led us to the door and pulled from his pocket a large key. He unlocked the door, took from his pocket a small flashlight and opened the door. It swung on its hinges without the theatrical squeal of rusty metal I expected. Fry's torch shone into a room empty but for a few heaps of sacking and crates and a lamp sitting on the floor.

"How did you get the key?" I asked.

"Connections," he said. "And the profession of scientist, which in these parts is still worth something. Mainly, I used the tower for an experiment that lasted several weeks."

We entered. Fry handed me the flashlight, pulled out matches, and, helped by the beam of the torch, raised the lamp's mantle and lit its wick. A soft light spread all around us and called from the dark rough walls and stairs leading to the next level.

"The duke lived here," Fry explained, moving towards the stairs. "The story is that he was afraid of someone or something and built the tower so he would be in a safe place and able to keep his eye on the countryside. Ironic, since he couldn't have hanged himself here if he hadn't built this place. A classical case of someone having no idea about the enemy in his own mind. After his death no one knew what to do with the monstrosity. It had a bad reputation and the living arrangements were not the most convenient."

Fry had stopped at the foot of the stairs. "I should warn you," he said. "I believe that this is potentially a dangerous place—I don't mean in terms of physical hazards, the floors and stairs are sound enough. But if you'd rather not go to the top . . ."

"After that lead-in?" Jim laughed. "Wild horses couldn't keep me from seeing the rest."

"Lead on, Macduff," Vida concurred.

I remained silent.

"What about you, John?" Fry asked.

I was cold and suddenly tired to the bone. But I said, "I don't believe in things that go bump in the night."

"Stout fellow," said Fry and headed up the stairs by the light of the lamp, telling us the story of the tower.

I was last. Looking at the wavering shadows cast on the walls by our little group and listening to Fry, I felt absurd to be in this place at this hour. The second-floor room was as empty as the first and, as Fry continued his story while we climbed through room after empty room, I mused at how appropriate the setting was for the mental desolation he was describing.

His story in essence was this: After the hanged duke had been cut down, few people had entered the tower for more than a hundred years. Then, in the middle of the nineteenth century, two lovers forbidden by their families to see each other had made a suicide pact. They would climb to the top of the tower and would cast themselves from it, hand in hand, leaving the world and all its cruelty—forever united in death. "The poor idiots," added Fry in an editorial aside. On a bitterly cold night they had fled from their homes and had met at a crossing. They had made their way to the tower shivering, probably holding on to one another, probably afraid someone would stop them before they were forever safe from a world that didn't understand. The door hadn't been locked then. They made their way to the top of the tower and must have stood there in cold terror at the thought of what they were about to do. But they straddled the balustrade, swung their legs over the black drop, and holding hands launched themselves into oblivion. Or rather one of them did. The boy. The girl at the last instant pulled her hand out of his—an instinctive reflex of self-preservation, understandable, forgivable, but he fell to his death, and she remained alive, fled down the stairs, kept fleeing.

We had arrived at a room that was not empty: it had a desk and chair, books and papers on both, a second desk with a computer, and, in a corner, a generator. "My study," Fry explained. "When I was doing my experiment. I still haven't cleaned up."

"What happened to the girl?" I asked.

"The coward," Vida corrected me.

"According to local lore she got married to a rich man and had a child, but on cold winter nights she heard her lover calling her from the tower, and one night, five years to the day after his death, she obeyed his call, ran to the tower and threw herself from the top. Her joining him in the hereafter seems to have satisfied the ghost; there is no evidence of anyone else having been driven to self-destruction by it."

"Served her right," Vida said. "You don't promise to stick with somebody and then change your mind when it counts."

The stairs ended at a trap door in the ceiling, and Fry led the way and used his shoulder to force it open. "Wait till you see how far down it looks from up here," he told Vida. "It's not difficult to see how you might lose your nerve."

The top was a square surrounded on all four sides by a

parapet. I moved over to the closest side, took one look down, at a vertiginous drop onto rocky soil, and feeling dizzy pulled back and kept my eyes on the surrounding country of shrubs and clumps of trees looking frozen and staged in the light of the moon.

"What intrigues me is that this is the end of the story," Fry said. "You'd think that the local imagination is sufficiently fertile to have come up with a continuance. Why not call it *La Torre degli Amanti*, The Tower of the Lovers, and have a girl throw herself off it every so often—or a boy for that matter? Why not at least hear the specters' mournful cries on the anniversary of their deaths?"

"Maybe the ghost was happy once his love joined him," Jim suggested. "Maybe the local imagination wanted a happy ending."

"Possibly," Fry agreed. "But it could also be that they always thought of the tower as an evil place and the people perishing in and around it as only accidental victims. They call it *La Torre del Diavolo*, very romantic—The Tower of the Devil."

Although the ache behind my eyes had become a steady throb and I felt dead tired, I couldn't resist introducing a rational note in all this melodrama. "That makes sense, since the duke killed himself long before the two lovers," I said.

"Exactly," Fry agreed. "Still, it does seem interestingly unimaginative in a country where everyone believes in ghosts."

Before I could think of a reply, Jim suddenly called out theatrically, "Enough of this agony!" and placing one hand and the opposite foot on the railing boosted himself up, swung his other leg over the side and sat on the parapet, his feet dangling over the drop. My stomach quavered at the memory of how far away the ground was, but Vida said, "Showoff," and cavalierly followed his example and sat next to him.

I suspected Fry was in shock, and I said, "Pay no attention to them. She's a rock climber and they're both lunatics."

Fry did not respond but kept his eyes on Vida and Jim. I wondered whether he was afraid movement or sound might startle them and they might lose their balance. I was used to Vida's climbing stunts but thought that she and Jim were behaving like jerks in giving our host a fright. Before I could reassure Fry further, he quoted slowly, without taking his eyes off the pair, "Golden lads and girls all must, As chimney sweepers, come to dust."

I didn't know what to make of his oddness. "In the fullness of time, one hopes," I said.

He let out a small laugh, "Indeed."

Vida and Jim began wondering audibly whether a gleaming strip on the horizon was the ocean or whether the tower was too far from the coast.

Fry abruptly turned to me and said, "I want to show you something, John," and we left the two daredevils and went down the stairs. Fry placed the lamp on the desk and rummaged in one of its drawers. He pulled out a deck of cards, searched through it and drew from it a card and handed it to me. The picture on it was startling. It showed a tower at night being struck by a bolt of lightning. Two figures, one male, one female, were hurtling from its shattered top, head over heels, arms raised in terror. The inscription below the picture said, "La Torre."

I was baffled. "I thought the girl threw herself off the top years later," I said, thinking that the scene was a ghoulish depiction of Fry's story. Then a memory stirred. "Or is it a tarot card?" I asked.

"Yes," said Fry. "The Tower, symbol of change, restructuring, possibly chaos, catastrophe, ruin, possibly death—all depending on the other cards in the configuration."

Jim and Vida had joined us, tired of flaunting a daring that impressed no one. "I had a girlfriend once who believed in the tarot," Jim said. "She kept her deck in a silk scarf and let no one else touch it."

"Was she good at reading the cards?" Fry asked.

"I doubt it. Everything she predicted was always wonderful. Good news, changes for the better, love, prosperity, happiness—plus, we were going to get married. To each other."

"I thought you said she predicted changes for the better," Vida ribbed him.

Jim said, "Ha, ha," and took the card out of my hand and inspected it. "I don't think her tower looked as sinister as this one," he said. "Are there different versions of the cards?"

"There are indeed," Fry answered, taking the card from his hand and sliding it into the deck. "But by my theory only some are gateways to an invisible world."

My illness set in with a vengeance at about that time. I started shaking with cold, and the sense of distortion I had felt earlier turned everything I saw indistinct and everything I heard muffled. All I remember about the drive back to town is not being able to rid my mind of the phrase "invisible world" and of a connected image or dream: some colorful scene that teased me with a nagging sense of shapes moving just behind it, or within it, but being blocked from view by what was visible.

JIM QUARREL SAVED MY LIFE ON A BROWN FEBRUARY
afternoon. I remember the day as brown because mounds
of snow dirtied by exhaust fumes and road salt were all that
was left of the winter wonderland the city had been a few
days earlier after a blizzard had swept through it. Vida and I
had been to a movie, taking advantage of matinee prices. The
moment we left the theater, we got into one of those pointless arguments we were forever having at that time. I thought
the movie, a French film noir about a man hired to kill a
political figure who, unbeknownst to anyone, was the assas-
sin's father, was a black comedy; Vida understood it to be
utterly serious and steeped in moral ambiguity. I was bored
with the argument the moment it began, but the undercur-
rent of irritation that sucked on both of us day and night kept
me bringing up the numerous pieces of evidence that
showed, to anyone who didn't ignore a slew of obvious hints,
that I was right.

I knew (or thought I knew), and chose to ignore, the true

cause of our perpetually being at each other's throats. Ignoring the true cause, I responded only to Vida's new tendency to aggressively assert her own opinions on everything under the sun—from why the hero had become an obsolete concept in art with any degree of sophistication to what made research on people alive more likely to produce a good likeness than research on the defunct. A saint might have listened with forbearance to her pontificating over things I did, with all due respect for the new Master of Arts, know a bit more about than she. I was not a saint, and since I felt I had every right to be peeved, forbearance was in short supply around the house.

The grand plan had been for Vida to get a job in publishing as soon as she had her degree. She was going to quit being a part-time personal trainer at an athletics club and rejoin the humdrum world of nine-to-five employment, which she had left two years earlier when she'd given up on a dead-end job to go to graduate school. Instead she spent a few weeks unsuccessfully pounding the pavement—as I had predicted, an M.A. in the history of science did not make her the most desirable candidate for a career in publishing. Then, certainly long before she had investigated all possible avenues, she ran across an article, and it gave her an idea. She showed it to me, hardly able to contain herself with excitement. He— "he" being Geoffrey Fry—was the perfect subject for a book linking biography with the scientific ideas of the age, she announced. Her thesis on Lintot had provided her with the model on how to go about the project, and she was convinced that a book on the scientific mind was marketable.

She did not suggest that Geoffrey Fry might be more marketable than my great-uncle, but when I said I wasn't sure there would be enough human interest in someone like Fry and his esoteric ideas, she countered that maybe human interest was overrated. I said it had been a seller at least since Achilles sulked and Ulysses got in trouble with Circe, and we were off on our first row related to our parallel literary projects.

I thought her enthusiasm might wane when she realized that science had become a good deal more complicated since the days when Lintot spontaneously generated deathwatch beetles, and that writing about Fry would be difficult without a scientific background. But luck was with Vida. In the same journal in which she found the article on Fry was an announcement of grants for interdisciplinary projects linking science with the humanities. Vida applied, and eight anxious, nail-biting months later she was in possession of the princely sum of $10,000 to be used for travel, lodging, and living and miscellaneous expenses related to her project. She wrote to Fry in Italy, he wrote back, telling her he was willing to cooperate, and I talked myself into taking an unpaid leave from my main job with the idea of using those four weeks in Italy to get a sizable chunk of my book written. A few months later we were in Frascati.

Before that windfall we argued a great deal. My disappointment at being forced to continue holding two jobs to support us and seeing all of my time used up—I was lucky to hack out two pages a week—kept gnawing at me. I had planned to quit one job and settle into a less stressful and more productive routine as soon as she had her degree and a job, but once the idea of the book on Fry took hold of her, her job search became half-hearted and sporadic. What added to my perpetual irritation was that rightly or wrongly

I sensed in her the sentiment that since she had stayed with me stalwartly when my career had taken its fatal plunge, I owed her.

So we argued about things neither of us gave a damn about, and hurt ourselves and one another in the process, and I felt spiteful and hated myself for the feeling but couldn't shed it. As happened during that afternoon's idiotic argument after the movie.

We were heading down the street and were about to cross an intersection when from the out-of-nowhere in which things hover when one's mind is otherwise occupied, a figure rose up and I felt my arm grabbed. I tried to extricate myself from the grip but the massive bulk of a man bore down on me. His hair was long and stringy, and tiny red eyes peeked through strands of it. My face was in the hot reek of his boozy breath. He shouted at me something I didn't understand, something garbled and enraged. Then what he shouted became intelligible. "Nobody goes there! You understand? Nobody! Nobody! You don't go there!" In his free hand, the one that wasn't holding me close to him, was a linoleum knife, its rusty blade extended to its fullest. He raised it to the height of my face and I instinctively grabbed his hand at the wrist. "You're dead!" he shouted. "You're dead! You're dead! You're dead!" And he jerked his hand back and forth to break my hold.

I was struggling with him, shouting I don't know what, frantically looking around for help. There were plenty of people, the nearest Vida. She met my eyes with a startled, indecisive look. Other faces showed fear, embarrassment, bald curiosity. I shouted, "Get the police!" and fought to keep the rusty blade away from my face and throat. "Nobody!

You're dead! dead! dead!" the madman screamed at me and jerked the knife back and forth, left and right, as if he were following some choreographed set of moves while holding me like a partner in a dance.

Then a hand closed around his wrist and a forearm locked across his throat, and my rescuer, a young bearded man in a bomber jacket, said to the attacker, "Let go of the thing! Let it go!" The lunatic released his grip on me and tried to pull my rescuer's arm away from his throat, but Jim held on and now there were suddenly Vida and a policeman helping him, the knife fell on a frozen mound of snow and skidded down and stopped at my feet.

We had dinner with Jim Quarrel a few hours later. In the course of the conversation, we told him of the recent departure of our sublettee, an Indian graduate student. As it turned out, Jim had just broken up with his girlfriend and was apartment hunting. We described the studio tacked on to our apartment: separate kitchen and bathroom, but connected to our apartment through a door—someone's idea of an in-law unit for apartment living. Jim was interested, we showed him the place, and the next day our new renter moved in, carrying his belongings in a suitcase, a backpack and a duffel bag. We soon realized that Jim would become more than a casual acquaintance. He invited us to dinner at his place, twenty paces from ours; we reciprocated, and within a week we had a friend.

I liked Jim from the start in an unthinking way. He was pleasant and outgoing. He had come to my aid, and he shrugged off his action without false modesty as simply something that had been necessary—no great feat. Although he had quit college after two years he was well read and had in his head a surprising amount of information about things I had no reason to suspect him of knowing. One day he startled me by reciting two lines from Swift's notorious elegy on Marlborough: "From all his ill-got honours flung, Turn'd to that dirt from whence he sprung." He had traveled a good deal in Europe and could ask for the train station or nearest inn or bathroom in four or five foreign languages and conduct a semi-coherent conversation in two.

When we met him, Jim made his living as a cabbie. It was his fifth or so job in as many years—the one before had been to repair bus engines for the city, the one before to drive an armored truck—and there was no reason to believe he would stick with it. He quit it with alacrity when he found a way to get discount airplane tickets for himself and me so we could take a holiday with Vida, by visiting, in his enthusiastic version, *"La bella Italia, mamma mia, che gelida manina!"*

As I got to know Jim better over the months, I discovered some unsuspected qualities in him. During the first weeks of our acquaintance, there were moments of shyness that rendered him tongue-tied. Then, as I saw more of him, I became aware that he could be moved, sometimes to tears, by odd things: once I saw him watch a solitary young boy throw a ball against the wall of a building across the street and when he turned to me, his eyes were lustrous. I also discovered flashes of a sardonic temper and something I couldn't—or didn't bother to—put a finger on: now and then he'd look at me with a roguish expression out of the corner of his eye after saying something. It was as if he were checking whether

I got the joke or were telling me that he had an ace up his sleeve. I suppose that if I had tried at all, any prodding on my part would have made him open up to me and tell me a few startling things about himself—a part of his nature was an impulse toward the confessional. But if I ever thought of him as someone with a secret, I clearly felt that it was not my business to try to elicit it from him.

It must quickly have become obvious to our new friend that he had not stumbled upon the most harmonious of households. But he soon learned to stay out of the way when Vida and I were at each other's throat, and there were times when he was able to defuse an argument in the making by doing a British Bobby "What's all this then?" routine or some other theatrical tomfoolery that made us all laugh.

With respect to Vida, he turned out to be an even greater boon. She discovered in him a kindred spirit, someone sharing her interest in the great outdoors, wood and mountain lore, and general athleticism and derring-do. Jim knew how to rappel off high places, start a fire with sticks of wood, protect himself in a snowstorm by building a snow cave; he also could do seventy pushups (compared to Vida's twenty-five and my twelve—we had a prowessfest one evening after too much to drink), could run five miles in the park keeping up with Vida, and do a four-minute handstand (Vida's record was fifty seconds).

When he and Vida first began doing things together, I sensed that he was afraid I might think of him as a potential or would-be rival. He was, after all, only two years older than she; I, fifteen years older, must have seemed to him to be approaching senescence in sexual terms. But it was clear to me that Vida considered him a pal, a fellow jock, someone in whom she had not the slightest physical or romantic interest but with whom she enjoyed running and playing handball and Frisbee golf, activities that bored me. Her lack of interest in Jim as an "eligible male" explains why I felt no prickles of jealousy when they spent time alone together and nursed no suspicion of any hidden agenda according to which he was trying to get into her pants and/or heart. I was genuinely glad—and Jim must have quickly recognized my feelings—that she had found a friend with whom she could follow the athletic leanings that made her the young, fleet-footed, impetuous love of my life. That in Jim she found a friend to whom she felt closer than to me in at least one crucial respect, I found out almost too late.

I woke up in the early morning from a dream in which my head was being sucked into a jet engine. There was a pounding ache behind my eyes and a dull pain in my joints. I was also furiously thirsty. After crawling out of bed and drinking greedily from the bathroom tap, I looked in the mirror at a ghost: black hollows for eyes, the sunken cheeks of a long illness. I had to hold on to the wall to make my way back to bed, and nearly collapsed before reaching it. I don't know whether I deliberately woke Vida or groaned impressively enough to wake her. All I remember is that throughout the next week I was fully conscious only a fraction of the time and lived otherwise in a gray land of ache and violent discomfort. Awareness became shards of sights and sensations packed in cotton wool: a tall silver-haired gentleman leaning over me and saying things in an unintelligible language to somebody else in the room; swallowing with a raw throat bitter lemonade kept on my nightstand, or spoonfuls of broth ladled into my mouth by Vida; oceans of a clear watery liquid pouring out of my nose into tissue after tissue I wadded under my face; a steady ebb and tide of sleep and half-sleep, being alone in the dark (Vida, I found out when I recovered, had moved into Jim's room and he into the living room because she couldn't get any sleep with me groaning and coughing all night). I had a recurring dream of a tower growing into the earth instead of out of it and was troubled and pained by this tube poking into the ground like a wound. Once, in the middle of the day, I woke up and jumped out of bed, and trembling with weakness stood leaning against a chest of drawers thinking that I had to do something to save Vida. I had to save her, or protect her, or do something to keep from losing her forever. I stood, gripped by a desperate sense of urgency until I became more awake and weakness and dizziness made me crawl back into bed.

After a week I began to feel better, was able to eat solid food and shuffle about in the apartment and through the small garden of stubby olive trees at the back of the villa. I had returned to the land of the living, but I was in the curious position of being a stranger in an exotic land that held no mystery for my companions. It was as if I had joined late a regiment that had been posted to foreign shores. During that week of my absence, Vida and Jim had become old Frascati hands. They knew where the two supermarkets were and which one had the better produce; they knew where to get spit-roasted chicken, inexpensive but good wine, the best pizza in town, what the stationery stores had to offer; they joked about their dictionary conversation with a pharmacist at the place where they had bought my cold medicine; and their talk was sprinkled with Italian words: the pharmacy was the *farmacia*, chicken was *pollo*, the young bank guard at the top of the road, who was always eager to give directions, the *guardia*.

They had also settled into a routine. Jim had met an American who was building a house outside Frascati, and the man had hired him to help with the concrete work. Vida saw Fry daily at the Institute and followed him wherever he went (like a Golden Retriever, Jim said when she was out of the room). She was energetically committed to her project and talked about Fry animatedly in the evening. Her exuberance tired me, but my enfeebled condition would have made any display of excessive energy seem wasteful. Maybe my sense of dislocation or alienation had more to do with a lingering lack of vitality than with anything else, but if I had been unenthusiastic about the trip before, I now felt that coming to Italy had been a bad idea, and I began counting the days until we'd be back in New York.

The first day I felt stronger I decided to take a walk. Vida offered to accompany me, but I knew her idea of a leisurely walk—a forced march to ordinary mortals—and told her I'd be fine tottering up the road on my own. She stayed at the villa, organizing her notes. Jim watched a Sunday Mass he had found on TV, fascinated by a pomp and spectacle that he, a lapsed Presbyterian, hadn't dared to dream.

The sun was a white wafer behind the clouds, and I felt cold the moment I left the villa. I hadn't gotten far up our narrow one-way street, walls hiding gardens or houses on either side, and was already wondering whether it wouldn't be wise to head back, when a fast car behind me suddenly slowed to my crawl and Fry lowered the window. "How about a ride?" he asked. "Are you sure you ought to be out and about?"

I told him that I was conducting a test of my stamina, which was, now that the results were in, not excessive.

He said, "You haven't even seen the town. Get in and I'll give you a quick tour before we bundle you off to bed again."

I got in, and he drove up to the main piazza, explaining that by car one had to take the roundabout way, but there was a shortcut up a long stair. He sympathized with me for so far having had a lousy time of my Italian holiday. "I hope things will be better from now on," he said. "The country has a lot to offer if you're not deathly ill. And I'd like to see more of you." He gave me a quick look from the side, but his eyes were back on the road by the time I turned my head, and I wondered whether he had checked my reaction to the evidence that a man of his eminence could be so solicitous to a stranger. "Vida has told me a lot about you," he continued. "It's high time I get it from the horse's mouth."

I was about to point out that there was singularly little to tell (it was unlikely she had mentioned the signal event of my life, "The Great Scandal"), but we drove past the Villa Aldobrandini, a stately manor lording it over the town, and Fry provided guidebook-type details about dates, people and features. Then he parked the car and took me down a short road to the Piazza del Duomo and explained its dome and church.

I was more interested in the people. The streets and squares were crowded with families in their Sunday best, the women almost without exception wearing furs, the men leather jackets or heavy wool coats. But the small children that were everywhere had on elaborate costumes of silk and velvet. I saw miniature Zorros and princesses and court jesters and Napoleonic soldiers. "It's *carnevale*," Fry explained. "The tykes get to show off their masquerade finery every Sunday during the season. Note that there is no comparison to our Halloween costumes. Most of these getups are hand-sewn from high-quality fabrics. Cute as a bug's ear." He point-ed at a diminutive harlequin in green and pink satin and a jester's cap, and his sister, a slightly taller harem beauty com-plete with billowing lilac trousers and silver veil.

We returned to the car and drove a short distance to what was formerly the garden of a villa but was now open to the public. Fry parked the car and we slowly walked up a steep incline and on top leaned on a low wall to observe the Sunday strollers below. The sun was stronger now and gave everything color.

"I'm never quite sure the children enjoy it as much as the parents are pleased to think they do," Fry commented in response to the sudden tearful outburst of a pint-size Fred Astaire who had both parents huddling like mother hens. "And of course everyone's oblivious of the fact that the spir-it remains pagan no matter how much Mother Church has tried to fold the concept into its ample corpus and wrap bare-assed Dionysus in Christian robes. The meaning remains the same: the renewal of nature, birth after death, masks, riot, licentiousness to quicken wombs. Here the bigger kids have shaving-cream fights, they spray each other with the stuff. All very controlled, no maenads hunting their quarry to the ground and tearing him to pieces." Then, with no hint of a transition, and without taking his eyes off the pageantry below, Fry asked, "What do you think of my theory of coincidence?"

"I haven't had a chance to think about it, or anything else for that matter," I said. "The world has been a fog."

"No doubt, but there is a reason I'm bringing it up. Tell me what you see down there?"

I saw nothing but several groups of Sunday strollers. Fred Astaire had had his tears dried and was smiling for a video camera held by his father. "People," I said.

"OK, dumb question. What do you see right in front of us?"

I looked. "You mean what is most striking? The kids: a pirate, a fairy, a Fred Astaire who seems to have recovered his cheery disposition."

"What do they have in common? In other words, what is the coincidence?"

I took a closer look. The six- or seven-year-old pirate wore crimson velvet knickers, a white silk shirt and a black velvet vest. He had an eye patch, a three-cornered hat and carried his rapier in a golden sash. Fred Astaire was maybe four, and was, in agreement with Fry's judgment, cute as a bug's ear in full evening dress of tails and shiny top hat, and cane in one white-gloved hand. The fairy was eight or nine and in shimmering pink satin and gold-lamé cloak and silver slippers. That she was a fairy rather than a princess was made clear by her magic wand with a crystal star on top.

"Their costumes look expensive," I tried. "And the kids all look self-conscious."

Fry shook his head. "All the costumes look expensive and all the kids are self-conscious."

"Then I don't see the coincidence."

"How about that each of them carries a rod-shaped object? Rapier, magic wand and cane."

Fry's case seemed weak to me. I said, "But don't we have to find out now how many of all the costumes have rod-shaped objects as part of the getup? Suppose it's eighty percent?"

"It isn't," Fry said. "But you're still not looking. Look at the parents."

The two boys were accompanied by both parents; the girl by a man, presumably her father. Of the two women, one wore a full-length fur, the other a leather coat trimmed with fur. Of the men, two wore leather jackets, the third a woolen coat. They all seemed to be of roughly the same age. "I don't see anything," I said. "They're all probably in their thirties, if that means anything."

"You're not looking," Fry said.

The pirate and his entourage, taking their cue from Fred Astaire, had stopped for a photo session; the father and his fairy daughter were on their way back to the car. Then I saw it: he was wearing a long plaid scarf, and so were the fathers of the two boys. "The scarves," I said.

"Bingo," Fry said and slapped me on the back. "Welcome to the world of coincidence. And let me just add that tartan scarves are not an integral element in the local dress code."

On the drive back to the villa, we saw the man and his fairy daughter again. They had been in an accident with a motorcycle. The cycle lay in front of their car in a mess of debris from a broken headlight. The daughter was sitting in the car, while her father and other people were bent over a boy of fifteen or sixteen sitting on the curb and holding a blood-soaked handkerchief to the side of his head. The boy was wearing a Tarzan costume of leopard-spotted loincloth over flesh-colored tights and leotard.

Fry carefully maneuvered the car around the scene.

I said, "That must have happened just a few minutes ago. The man and the kid were in the park."

Fry didn't reply, and I wondered whether he'd heard me. Then he asked, "Are you afraid of death?"

I was startled by the abruptness of the question. "Sure," I said. "It's not something I spend an enormous amount of time thinking about, but sure. Why do you ask?"

"That small reminder of mortality back there. A slightly more forceful encounter of his head with whatever it encountered and he might be dead. It's the most amazing thing under the sun, isn't it? One moment you're here, the next you're gone."

"Into that silent land," I quoted, unable to think of anything else to say.

Fry looked at me from the side. "How afraid are you of death, those times when you do think about it?"

"Depends. Right now not very. It seems too abstract an idea, too remote or unlikely. The sun is out, the town is lively and full of color. I love those salmon-pink buildings and the mixture of old and new architecture everywhere. It seems absurd to be thinking of death."

"If that boy had died back there, he'd be seeing nothing of any of this, and there'd be nothing in the least abstract about his being dead. Although in that costume of his he would look absurd."

His morbidity was starting to make me uncomfortable.

"True, but that thought doesn't make it any easier for me to project myself into a state of mortal terror now."

"Of course. Reason is your middle name, isn't it? Unless you feel a bony hand on your shoulder and a cold breath on your neck, what's the point of shivering in your boots, right? Stay away from the charnel house and all's well."

"Something to that effect."

"But I take it you do remember how you felt when you thought that madman was going to slit your throat. When you thought you might die?"

"If I have to."

Fry laughed an aggressive laugh. "Gloat not, proud death! Though you lay your icy hand on kings, John Anders knows you only by an act of will."

I started protesting that I was not that arrogant, but we had arrived at the gate of the villa and Fry interrupted me. "Don't be a fool. Use whatever resources you have in the battles you fight. Even in those you're bound to lose."

I said that that didn't seem the most economical approach to the expenditure of one's resources, but he ignored the joke, told me to say hello to Vida and Jim and drove off.

Walking up the short driveway, I heard voices, Vida's and Jim's, behind the villa, and although I was tired enough to collapse after my grand tour of Frascati and bizarre argument—if that was what it had been—with Fry, I went around the house to investigate.

I found them entertaining themselves with something that looked like a mix between a medieval crossbow and an Uzi:

a short "barrel," a pistol grip, and an arrow protruding with an ugly barbed triangular tip. It was a spear gun, they informed me. Vida had found it and two arrows—or were they called spears?—in a closet behind brooms and mops. After they had cleaned it, its giant rubber band propelled the arrows with impressive force across the lawn. They had gotten a large cardboard box, drawn a bull's-eye on one of its sides, and were using it for target practice. Part of the garden was an elevated terrace, reachable by a few worn marble steps, and they shot the hissing projectiles from there, so arrows missing the target planted themselves in the surrounding leaf-covered lawn rather than in the neighbor's overgrown garden. The distance from which they fired made them miss the target more often than they hit it, and since there were only the two arrows, both of them did a good deal of running back and forth to retrieve them.

Watching my two dear idiots firing their weapon, letting out Apache whoops when an arrow embedded itself in the box with a dull *thunk*, I thought, Fry would love them: more coincidental rod-shaped objects for his daily collection. And at least some attempt at make-believe even if the braves had refrained from smearing their faces with war paint.

I don't know whether my watching them made them self-conscious or whether in my enfeebled state any unnecessary use of energy would have struck me as forced, but I had the distinct impression of something phony about their playful tomfoolery. It was as if they were pretending to enjoy something they had no real interest in.

I was about to leave them to their strenuous fun, when an arrow fired by Vida went wide. It struck the trunk of an olive tree flanking the line of fire with a sharp clang and broke off at the tip—the shaft bouncing off the tree with a high ring and landing in the grass. Jim trotted up to the shaft and inspected the break. "It's solid steel," he told me. And for the benefit of the mechanically obtuse, he added, "Must have had a flaw at the weld." He tried to free the tip, but it was too firmly embedded in the tree and not enough of it protruded for him to get a good grip on it. He called to Vida, "We're running low on ammo. How about surrender?"

"Never!" she called back, and after Jim had moved a safe distance away from the tree, she shot the remaining arrow squarely at the box and it struck close to the bull's-eye.

I told them I was going to bed and to please keep it down to a roar. By the time I had drunk a glass of water in the bathroom and gotten undressed, they had come in and were being quiet in the living room. I was allowed to glide into sleep undisturbed, and I slept, lost to all clues, internal or external. At least for the moment, the gate of horn, portal of prophetic dreams, had been barred against even the most urgent warning from the future.

Was I superstitious before our Italian adventure? The casual observer would have said no. I did not believe in lucky or unlucky numbers, jinxes, hexes, omens or fetches. And yet, as I realize now, I was abjectly superstitious about one area of my life, and superstitious fear was as much to blame for what happened, or did not happen, between me and Vida in five years of marriage as her own reluctance to let me know her. My superstition appeared in response to certain situations and took the form of a sudden, intense feeling of alarm—a voice whispering: "Careful now. Don't move. Don't look. Don't ask." And I acted accordingly, with caution, afraid the ground would open and I would be hurled into deepest night if I made a mistake now.

Twice in my life—once when I was four, once when I was seventeen—the urge to know something made me open a private Pandora's box and I was punished to a degree so greatly exceeding the transgression that it was laughable to think of what happened in terms of crime and punishment. If I had peeked through an off-limits crack in a curtain and been deprived of an eye for it, the match between deed and retribution would have been no worse. But on some visceral, untouched-by-reason level, I did perceive it in those terms and became fearful of certain impulses, and protected myself by unthinkingly erecting barriers—my equivalent of the instinctive crossing of fingers or making a detour around ladders.

When I was four I loved my grandmother above all things on earth. She was my dearest. I'd heard the term in a movie and once told her with great solemnity—referring to a wooden puzzle that had me stymied—"I can't make this work, my dearest." She laughed out loud, a sudden burst of gladness and gaiety that warmed me to the core, and from then on I often called her my dearest when we were alone. She called me Joba, and I never lost my delight at hearing her say this special name she had found for me and was the only one to use. The terms of endearment were part of a private language we had, a language composed of lines from movies we saw together and from favorite comic books I showed her. It was a code of affection that could have me in stitches when she or I matched one of its expressions with something we observed or talked about, and there was a special thrill in the knowledge that only the two of us understood the joke.

How often in his life does anyone encounter love that is unreserved, unquestioned, unconditionally given? I encountered it in my grandmother. There was an understanding between us, an instinctive, spontaneous liking from my first memory of her. I loved being with her, and she, a writer of tales of fantasy whose heroes were forever battling nefarious foes on distant worlds, enjoyed having me around and gladly baby-sat for my working parents. They were afraid I'd get on her nerves and could never quite believe that I really was no trouble at all, was happy to let her write while I played with my toys or looked at my picture books until she sat down and played with me or read to me from what she had written. Or we'd talk. I felt I could talk to her about anything, and she'd tell me stories about her life and I'd catch fascinating glimpses of the mysterious world of adults.

My father joked that we were soul mates and had been sweethearts in a previous life. But I thought that we were sweethearts now and that I'd want no other. She was beautiful, with raven hair and large green-brown eyes the color of a brook in a heather. I liked to look at her, and I remember moments of surpassing happiness seeing her ponder a page before her and knowing that she was my dearest.

But she became ill and had to go to the hospital for an operation to remove a tumor (a word that seemed to me more sinister than any other I knew because it sounded like *humor* and meant the opposite). The operation was on her brain. When she came back she was thinner and still had to stay in bed. My father took time off from work to take care of me and spell the hired nurse at my grandmother's house. One late afternoon my mother was at home with me when he called from there. It was getting dark and there was snow on the ground. My mother bundled me up and we drove to my grandmother's house, where my father, upset and haggard-looking, said he couldn't get hold of the nurse, had called the doctor, but it had all happened so fast. They told me to stay in the living room and went into my grandmother's bedroom. I knew that a vast catastrophe had befallen me but was afraid to think about what it was. Then an uncle and aunt were at the door and my parents came out of the bedroom to talk to them.

And I, left unattended, went down the hall and stood outside the bedroom door listening. When there was no sound, I opened the door and went inside. A single lamp on a dresser was lit against the gloom of early evening. Someone—I knew it had to be my grandmother—lay on the bed under blankets and a sheet. The sheet had been drawn over her head. I didn't want to but couldn't help myself and went to the side of the bed. I also didn't want to, and knew it was wrong, but had to see what was under the sheet. I pulled it down and saw her face, saw her, staring with eyes wide open and sightless at a corner of the room.

Then my father swept me up in his arms and carried me into the living room, and my mother sat with me in a corner and told me about how Gran wasn't really gone but was in heaven looking down on me, and that it was all right if I wanted to cry. I shouldn't try to be brave. Crying would make me feel better. And I started to cry to reassure her.

But the damage had been done and there was no undoing it. The signs were large and small. One was that for more than twenty-five years I could remember my grandmother's face only as a photograph on a wall, a portrait in which she smiled formally at the viewer; it took the discovery of a photo album with snapshots of her to make me remember what she had looked like. Another was nightmares. Years after her death I still had dreams in which I ran terrified through the rooms of a house with no exit, pursued by something that was and wasn't my grandmother, something dreadful, inhuman, dead. Yet another sign of the damage was the fact that for an eternity I had no deep feelings for anyone. It wasn't that I was unhappy. I was fond of my parents. But that feeling of a rare gladness, that blending of delight, harmony and ease that I had felt in my grandmother's company was gone, and even my memory of it seemed to have been erased.

A coda to all this was that when some ten years ago my grandmother's death came up in a talk I had with my father, he claimed that the traumatic scene I remembered had never happened. Yes, I had been at the house that afternoon, but I had not set foot in the bedroom. My mother and I had arrived at the same time his brother's car had pulled up in the driveway, and my mother and aunt had stayed with me in the living room while his brother and he had gone into the bedroom. So it is possible that I committed the great dreadful crime of my childhood entirely in my mind, in a hallucination or a dream—the details of gloom at the window and lit lamp provided by memory, my ghastly discovery of what was under the sheet by imagination. An ironic turn, if true, but the new insight had no effect on my habits of mind.

For an eternity of eight years after my grandmother's death I had no deep feelings for anyone. Then, when I was twelve, a miracle happened. A boy named Will Barnaby became my desk mate in junior high school and soon, and with no effort at all, my friend. The magic hand of chance put at my right elbow someone to love, and it did the same for Will at his left elbow. For five years, he and I lived in a state of grace. In five years, in which we went through puberty and adolescence, in which we saw each other almost daily, we never once had a single argument. Even our rare disagreements never lasted for more than a few hours. Our tempers, interests, likes, dislikes were matched so perfectly that we had a near-telepathic sense of what the other was thinking, feeling, in the mood to do. We were both bookish, and we read the same stories, found the same things funny, liked the same movies, even had the same favorite ice cream: peppermint and chocolate. We were both shy of girls and only marginally interested in sports. There were only two things in which we differed markedly. One was our looks. I was black-haired and big-boned and had features too rough ever to be considered handsome; he was blond and slim, and he slipped with nary a ripple from attractive boyhood into attractive adolescence. The other thing in which we differed was our home life. Mine was stable and without drama; he had a lunatic older sister and parents wholly wrapped up in her. His sister, forever in and out of institutions, would every so often terrify the family with a half-hearted suicide attempt, or she'd write dirty limericks on the living-room walls with colored felt-pens, or break her father's records and tapes. As a result, Will was not allowed to bring home anyone. We had been friends for several years before I saw his house, and then only from the outside. When for some forgotten reason I picked him up there one day, he pointed to an upstairs window at the side and told me his room was there. The house looked unremarkable if somewhat unkempt, but I wondered what the inside was like with the lunatic prowling about. I did get a partial answer to my question on the last day of our friendship, the day I climbed a tree and looked through the window into Will's room.

No event of truly ruinous consequences ever occurs as the result of a single thing. It takes a juxtaposition of actions, objects, and responses to what happens to make a disaster. If

Will's parents and his sister hadn't been away on that day, all would have been well. Or if he hadn't told me that they were away, or if I hadn't thought that we'd be visiting an aunt on that day, or if an old school chum of hers hadn't paid her a surprise visit, which had meant a call from her and a change of plans. Or if a tree hadn't stood at the side of Will's house where his room was. Remove any one of these items from the list and Will and I are still friends, keeping in touch through letters and phone calls—true friends for life. Keep two additional items, my wanting to surprise him at his home and my curiosity about its inside, off the list and no harm is done.

But all of these things appeared on my checklist for disaster, and shortly before noon on that day, I stood before Will's house and rang the doorbell. I waited but nobody answered, and I was disappointed at my surprise having been foiled. The drawn curtains didn't allow a peek, so I couldn't even satisfy my curiosity. After a few minutes of waiting for Will to come back from wherever he had gone off to, I started walking away. But then I noticed the leafless birch at the side of the house, in front of Will's open-curtained window, and decided on the spur of the moment to climb it to look into his room. At eye level with the window, I saw nothing out of the ordinary: a bed, small desk, bookshelf; a large poster of the Parthenon—a Christmas present from me—on a wall.

Then Will came in through a bathroom door, Will dressed in a brassiere, panties, garter belt, nylon stockings and high heels. And Will looked at the window and saw me.

I don't remember getting down from the tree or what I did after I got down. I do remember talking to him either later that day or the next day, somewhere in a park. Telling him it didn't matter to me if he was gay. He told me in a flat voice that he wasn't gay and didn't want to talk about what had happened. I kept saying, like a soul in hell still hoping words would buy a reprieve from everlasting damnation, that nothing mattered, I didn't care, nothing had changed between us, nothing would change. He said in that same flat voice that it was all right, everything was fine, he just didn't want to talk about it. But I knew that I had lost him for all time and would never again get him back.

We both did try. But what he thought I thought of him, or what I thought he thought I thought of him, was forever between us. The ease we had felt in one another's company, that sense of unexamined, unconscious harmony, was gone. We saw less and less of each other, and when we went off to different colleges a year later, I was relieved to lose a constant reminder of what I had robbed myself of in one instant of reckless curiosity.

I wonder now what Fry would have said if I had told him about the two catastrophic events of my childhood. He would, of course, have seen the obvious connections, from the profound to the trivial: both involved people I loved, both had to do with wanting to know, both took place in winter. He probably would have said, Beware of what you find out about those you love, especially in winter. But it took no systematic inquiry into coincidence for me to reach a similar conclusion—although I made no special effort to be uncurious only in winter.

✳

No magical sense of harmony or spontaneous liking accompanied my first encounter with Vida. She annoyed me, and she knew it. I was teaching a two-hundred-student survey course, Renaissance through Enlightenment, and had posted sign-up sheets, a slot for each half-hour increment, on my door to make my office hours less chaotic. The day on which I first saw my future wife as more than a face in a crowd, she was waiting for me in the corridor. She sat on the floor, next to my office, her legs crossed, an open book on them. Her flaxen hair was in a ponytail, she wore little or no makeup and was dressed in jeans and a gray sweatshirt. She closed her book and with the ease and grace of an athlete rose to my height. I greeted her, and checking the list on the door asked her whether she was Michelle someone-or-other. She said no, she hadn't signed up, and followed me into my office. I was about to tell her that she couldn't simply preempt somebody who had signed up and should be here any moment, but she said this wouldn't take long, put her backpack—a large scuffed thing with worn leather patches—on a chair, and extracted from it a few stapled-together sheets. She handed them to me and asked me to look at the paper and tell her what I thought.

My mood took a rapid dip. The top of the page gave me her name, Vida Morse, and told me that the essay had been written for one of the sections. I assumed I was in the presence of the usual student gripe about an unfair grade the teaching assistant had given her. She had handed me a fair copy without grade or comments. After telling her that she would have to leave when the student who had signed up appeared, because the whole point of sign-up sheets was that students wouldn't have to waste time waiting outside my door, I read a barely passable discussion on Catherine de' Medici and the Huguenots. Before me were paraphrased passages from one of the textbooks, chunks of *Encyclopaedia Britannica*, everything shoddily connected, half digested, disorganized, full of grammatical errors. I finished and looked up into belligerent eyes. Reading my impatience correctly, their owner had not sat down, and she had the stance of someone ready for a fight. "What do you think?" she asked.

I decided that only a full frontal attack had any chance of dislodging her from the absurd notion that she had been victimized. "It's lousy," I said. "The worst paper I've read in a long time."

She wasn't discouraged. "What grade would you give it?" she asked, her blue eyes blazing at me.

"I'd have to look at it more carefully, but at a first glance I'd say a D-minus." I assumed the TA had given her the usual charitable C to keep her out of his hair, and I hoped this verdict from higher up would make her thank her lucky stars and go away.

But she was undaunted. She pulled out of her pack a folder and took from it the identical essay, this time with the TA's red grade and three or four scattered remarks. The grade was A-minus. I was startled and tried to hide it by leafing through the sheets. At a place where the entire argument consisted of a single, grammatically incorrect, sentence he had written "awkward," another scant paragraph was marked with "more?" The lengthiest instance of pedagogic feedback was found at the end: "Nice job."

"He does that with everybody's papers," she said. "Fine job, good job, nice work; it doesn't matter how bad the paper is. I finally wrote one as bad as possible to prove it."

I didn't know what to do. I knew her TA had failed his first-year comprehensive exam and would try again in the spring. I knew he was overworked—who wasn't with the teaching and course load of graduate school? I also knew that the department would not be ecstatic about an Assistant Professor blowing the whistle on possible incompetence in the people it assigned to teach undergraduates. Meanwhile Ms. Morse was eyeing me with an expression as stubborn as it was wary. For lack of a better idea, I asked her whether she had heard other students in the class complain about the grading being too lenient.

"Complain?" she said and let out a snort. "No. All they do is joke about it. One guy says he'll hand in a paper covered with four-letter words—see if that'll get him a 'nice job' or 'great job' or just 'good work.'"

Fortunately, a face at the open door announced the arrival of the student who had signed up. I told Vida Morse that I'd talk to the TA.

She said, "I hate being a tattletale. But I don't see why people like that should be in a Ph.D. program. When they can't even teach a section."

I neither agreed nor disagreed with her, but put her essays aside and asked the student at the door to come in. My feeling was that setting a trap for someone was several degrees more contemptible than being a tattletale, and I thought, What a screwed-up bitch you are, my dear.

I confronted Phil, the graduate student, the next day. I anticipated an argument, but his nervous smile and frightened eyes when I found him in his closet of an office told me at once that there would be no fight. His collapse was instant and complete. He scanned the essay and when he looked up, his eyes were brimming and his mouth quivered. Out came the whole story: the pregnant, neurotic wife who needed him to do everything, the colicky one-and-a-half-year-old, thirty-two students and their papers in the two sections he was teaching, studying again for the exam he had failed and writing essays for his classes until two in the morning every night. Sometimes he had maybe ten minutes to correct and grade fifteen papers. As he was talking, he started to cry and I suspected the tears came as much from the hope that I'd take pity on him and somehow get him out of this mess as from fear and exhaustion. But there was nothing I could do. I told him what he knew perfectly well: graduate school was an endurance test under the best of circumstances and anyone who burdened himself with additional responsibilities did so at his own risk. He became even more confessional: his wife was seven years older than he and wanted children now. He had told her it would be difficult but . . . He simply didn't know what to do anymore.

He was still crying, and I was beginning to feel acutely embarrassed by the whole scene. My impression of him was that he was average and would have had only a marginally successful career as a graduate student under the best of circumstances. He had, in blunt terms, bitten off more than he could chew, having neither the talent nor drive that might have allowed him to succeed against overwhelming odds. My main difficulty in sympathizing with him was that this was the most taxing time in my own academic career. I had the workload of three classes, each of which required separate preparation. I was also on a time-consuming and utterly useless committee, and was working every spare moment—which meant the hours between ten at night and one in the morning—on the book I had to publish to get tenure. Still, although not consumed by compassion, I suggested commonsense solutions. Could his wife stay with his or her parents until he was back on his feet scholastically? Could he borrow money from someone and do without teaching for a while? I must have suggested several other short-term solutions. Phil, who looked as underfed as exhausted, listened to me with the resigned expression of someone who knew that he would have to waste precious time on something that would be of no help to him at all. His answer to every one of my suggestions was no—one thing or another made it impossible. He had stopped crying, and when I ran out of things to say, he thanked me for my concern and apologized for his "outburst": He didn't know what had come over him; he'd work things out somehow.

I told him to let me know how. He avoided my eyes when saying goodbye to me.

In the afternoon I looked for Vida Morse during my lecture on The Wars of Religion. I found her in one of the front rows, dressed in sweatshirt, sweatpants and basketball shoes. I could see the latter because she had loutishly planted a foot in the gap between two seats in front of her. Like most people in a crowd, she clearly thought that the lone lecturer looking down from his platform onto a sea of faces couldn't possibly identify her. I was tempted to shatter her complacency by interrupting the lecture and asking her whether she'd like the management to serve popcorn with the main feature. Not that she wasn't a serious student. She took notes throughout the lecture and when she didn't, tapped her pencil against her lips in what seemed genuine attention.

In the week that followed, I kept waiting for repentant

Phil to report to me about a proposed solution to his problems. He didn't. Then I got a call from one of the department secretaries. Phil had come to her earlier in the day and had told her he was quitting school, and to tell everybody who needed to know. Since he had hinted that I was somehow involved in his decision, I had to explain a few days later to the chairman of the department my role in it, presenting Vida's essay as Exhibit A.

Vida, whom I for some reason expected to come and see me, didn't. In the ensuing weeks, she attended the lectures, usually in her unisex outfits but once in a stylish mauve dress, heels, silky gray hose (no foot planted on backrest that time). She also had golden hoops hanging from her earlobes, and her loosed hair cascaded down her shoulders. I had to admit she was attractive, but something about this sudden maturing was disagreeable. It was as if she were wearing a disguise, and I was again reminded that here was a creature who had set a trap for someone and had mercilessly moved in for the kill when her victim had been caught.

Three days later she was back in my office in jeans and sweatshirt, crying as if she had lost everything in the world, with no hope of recovery. The occasion? Phil had been struck by a car and seriously injured.

I had heard about the accident from a colleague and felt sorry for Phil in a that's-all-the-poor-bastard-needs way. But here was Vida crying, claiming over and over that it was her fault. If she hadn't said anything he'd be all right. If she hadn't written that stupid essay and shown it to me, he would have been fine.

"You see, he's one of those people for whom nothing ever works," she said, looking at me beseechingly. "They try so

58

hard. They kill themselves trying. But things always go wrong. Nothing ever comes out right. They're never smart enough, or at the right place, or know the right people. Or the people they know stab them in the back. They never have luck in anything."

I couldn't believe what I was hearing. My first impulse when she had started her melodramatic self-recrimination had been the thought that, yes, she certainly deserved part of the blame even if she was extravagantly overreacting. But there was so much passion in what she said, and such sincere grief in how she said it, that I quickly began to feel concern for her. I told her that none of this was her fault; she had simply pointed out a problem that needed to be addressed. But she kept shaking her head: No, Phil would have been all right, everything might have worked out if she hadn't done what she did. And now he might die. (In fact, he recovered and moved to New Jersey with his wife and by then two children and became a bank manager, as I discovered when I ran into him years later.)

Vida kept shaking her head while I was arguing that an accident could happen to anyone at any time—it didn't matter whether one was happy or unhappy, whether one's life was going swimmingly or miserably, things came out of the blue and that was that—and she barely let me finish before insisting that, no, Phil would have been fine if it hadn't been for her, and she could prove it: if he'd still been a TA, he would have been teaching his section when the accident happened. He wouldn't have been out in the street.

I said, "You can't accept blame for random events. For all you know he could have been in a fatal accident if he'd taken the subway to campus in order to teach his section."

She suddenly gave up arguing and sat small and drawn into herself in the chair opposite me, crying quietly. Her grief moved me. It was clear to me that, no matter how misplaced, it left her exposed and defenseless. She was suffering and I wanted to help her. I wanted her to be well. I wanted to take her into my arms and comfort her.

I did not take her into my arms but waited in silence while she cried softly. When after a while she wiped the back of her hand under her nose like a child, I offered her a box of tissues. She took one and blew her nose. "I'm sorry," she said. "I don't know where that came from."

"It doesn't matter where things come from as long as they have a chance to get out," I told her, hoping I wasn't sounding patronizing.

"That one certainly had a chance," she said, balling up the tissue and lobbing it deftly into the wastepaper basket. "Thanks for humoring me."

It wasn't a question of humoring her. I was glad she had come to talk, I told her.

She gave me a rueful look, "I don't know why I came. I thought you didn't like me."

"So did I," I said, and we both laughed.

That shared laugh, so minor a thing, made a forgotten gladness stir in me. I sat up and rubbed my eyes after a long sleep, and saw that someone had sat down opposite me and was smiling at me.

We talked for another hour, about school, her plans for the future, her ideas about the veracity of history. She was intelligent, observant, articulate and had a dry sense of humor. I liked her and could tell that she liked me. Before I had to leave for a class, we agreed to meet for coffee the next day. Not too many days later, I found myself checking on a syllabus the number of weeks to the end of the semester when the ethical roadblock of our student/teacher relationship would be gone and we'd be able to see more of each other.

Six months later Vida and I were in love, seeing a great deal of each other, spending nights together. I had never been deeply in love and was unfamiliar with the giddy sense of well-being—the what-a-wonderful-world-it-is feeling of the condition. But I was old enough and well-enough versed in the lore of romance to recognize the state I was in as transient and to know that the enormous pull I felt toward Vida, and the euphoria that took hold of me whenever I was with her or thought of her were no guarantees of permanence. Unless they were based on something that made up in constancy for what it lacked in ecstasy, we wouldn't last. This conscious knowledge and fear of the ephemeral nature of passion had the effect of making me alert to signs that what Vida and I felt was genuine affection for one another—that it was love that would last us a lifetime.

I found the first such sign on an excursion to a small town in upstate New York. One weekend I thumbed my nose at the pile of work on my desk clamoring to be done, and we took a bus and, after leaving our things at a bed and breakfast inn, spent a beautiful May day wandering down country lanes, enjoying the view of rolling green hills. At the end of the day, after dinner at a small Italian restaurant, we returned to the inn. The place was rustic, with an Early American decor we both thought hideous—for which uncharitable thought we were promptly punished. In the small, overdecorated room were two twin-size beds with carved maple headboards and legs. The beds had been pushed together, either to provide more space elsewhere in the room or to create the semblance of a single, ample bed. Blindly taking our cue from the management, Vida and I proceeded to make love at the center of this contraption.

Initially we encountered no problems. But as things progressed from mildly to pronouncedly energetic, I became aware of motion under us. The bed was inexorably separating at the middle, the two parts marching further and further apart to the rhythm of our lovemaking. I could feel Vida struggling to accommodate to the chasm widening under her, and I tried to cling to the mattresses. But once the gap had achieved a certain critical width, it grew rapidly.

Vida started to laugh under me, and as we slipped unstoppably between the beds, I too began to laugh—which my erection did not survive. Safely on the floor, I lifted myself off Vida, in the throes of mirth under me, and managed to extricate myself from between the two mattresses. I collapsed on one of the beds; Vida's head and shoulders appeared. She gasped, "Oh Lord, to be a fly on the wall!" and flopped down next to me.

Her arm was across my chest and her hot laughing breath was at my cheek. I rolled over and pulled her close, and we kept laughing and creating scenarios concerning the thoughtful management's various policies with respect to its guests: our room for unwed guests who had to be kept pure; the bridal suite with the beds screwed firmly to the ground. Then there was the Reckless Debauchery Suite, reserved for celebrity guests beyond the pale. It had the same setup as the bridal suite but the headboard of one bed was joined to the footboard of the other. Laughing, I held laughing Vida in my arms, and I thought, Yes, this will last. Yes, it will.

One thing about reckonings following disasters is that they make us remember early warnings that we blithely ignored at the time. During the first months of being in love with Vida, I had an emblematic dream. I was standing in a spring forest. Rays of sun broke through the foliage of young leaves, and light and shadow played on the ferny ground. I was entranced by the bright trembling greens everywhere. More than that, I felt a sense of great ease, as if I had come home from far away to a place I loved. But the scene changed, grew brown and somber. I became afraid and turned to run away. Then I was in a grove, in it the statue of a woodland nymph—a beautiful girl, graceful and wild, garlanded with flowers of bright jade. I knew in my dream that I had arrived at a place of eternity where all things would forever stay the same. My fear left me and I felt an intense happiness, pure and undiluted.

The memory of that intense happiness and the scene connected with it stayed with me until the time came when I was forced to see the dream as an unsubtle jab by my subconscious meant to alert me to a sizeable flaw in the way I related to my future wife in psychological terms.

Another thing about disasters is that they make us sensitive—after the bodies have been collected and the events untangled—to signs of their meaning that we would otherwise have passed by without noticing. A few months ago I encountered one such sign. I was browsing in a used-book store and came across a collection of fairy tales and other stories of the supernatural. I randomly began reading a story and kept reading it mouth agape, not knowing whether to laugh or cry. I thought of Vida and Fry and Jim, and the coincidence that smacked me in the face by presenting me with this of all cautionary allegories.

In the story, a woman has a son, a beautiful little boy with a voice that is like the song of a bird and a great sweetness of disposition. He is his mother's happiness and she loves him to distraction. But one day she sees her little son try on a glue-on mustache in the mirror and she becomes afraid that he won't always be the way she loves him. She tells her sister about her fear, and the sister, a witch who has long been envious of her for having such a lovely child, tells her of an herb that, if plucked at midnight and placed on her son's brow, will make him stay forever the way he is now. The mother follows her advice, finds the herb and puts it on her sleeping son's brow. In the morning she tries to wake him, but she cannot. He stays asleep all day and all the following night and day. Day after day, week after week, he sleeps. His mother, in despair, goes to her sister for help. Her sister laughs at her and says: "You fool, how else did you think he could remain forever unchanged? Did you think he could go on living in the world and seeing and hearing, and remembering what he sees and hears, and never change? You got what you wanted. Be happy. He'll be this way all the days of your life."

The story continued for several more pages to what I assumed would be some magical solution to the problem, but the owner of the small store told me he was closing, and

I paid for the books I had picked and left without reading the happy ending.

I had had several medium-term relationships with women before Vida, but I hadn't lived with anyone. But I doubt cohabitation with a procession of women would have prepared me for the surprising pleasures of day-to-day life with Vida. There was, for instance, her attitude about nudity, a cavalierness that startled and delighted me. During our first hot, muggy summer together, I discovered that after taking a shower, she was prone to run around the apartment in gym shorts and nothing else. The sight of her lissome bare torso and small, carmel-brown-tipped breasts instantly aroused me, and we'd make love impromptu. My wife also thought nothing of sitting naked in a sauna after a long run, surrounded by other sweating naked bodies, male and female. I sometimes joined her, decorously clad in swimming trunks, my eyes chastely averted from the rampant nakedness of others but straying lovingly to her. I had seen her unconcerned attitude toward the exposed human form only in a college locker room: jocks stripping to the buff and padding off to a room full of showers in which no partitions separated the sudsy bodies. I'd demurely soap my chest while my neighbor would energetically lather groin and thighs and would scratch his rear on his way back to his locker, his towel nonchalantly draped over his shoulder.

Vida also had the athlete's lack of inhibitions about being touched. When she pulled a hamstring muscle during the one climbing trip on which I tagged along (I stayed at the base camp and read while she and others were ascending a rock wall), one of her fellow climbers, male and burly, expertly massaged the back of her bare thigh, stopping just short of the bikini panties she had stripped to. I looked on, charmed by the innocence of the act.

By the time I met Vida, she was no longer climbing mountains on most summer weekends. But two or three times a year she still went climbing in the Adirondacks, laughing at my apprehension and somber reminders that she had broken an ankle in a climbing accident—what if it had been her head? A week later, I'd be looking at heart-stopping photos of her on a sheer wall a hundred feet up, a thin nylon line the only backup if a rock should break loose under her foot.

I never asked myself why she courted danger, or why the danger she courted was of a kind she could train for and exert considerable control over. Now I see her mountain climbing as a symbolic quest for invulnerability—a subconscious recognition that she had been hurt and a desire to protect herself from future hurt and injury. But in those days, I was unwilling to consider that eccentricity as anything other than part of the child-of-nature package I had gotten and made no attempt to understand it.

Another thing I made no attempt to understand was why, despite an outward appearance of almost instinctive candor, there was a reserve at the core of Vida, an ultimate barrier to intimacy, as obvious to me as a no-trespassing sign. And yet, there were times during our first years of marriage when she'd cling to me wordlessly, gripped by some powerful emotion. I would ask her dutifully what was the matter, but she wouldn't answer; she would hold on to me, and I'd say nothing else, afraid that if I prodded or probed, she would tell me what was the matter and in doing so would ruin all there was between us. It seems obvious now that at those times she desired to be asked, asked with insistence and concern, what was going on inside her so she could answer, and maybe in answering fight her demons, and maybe in fighting them put them to rest. But a voice whispered into my ear: "Be careful, don't look, don't ask!" and I obeyed it and kept quiet. A correlative of my fear of discovering what I was not meant to discover was that I knew next to nothing about Vida's childhood or her parents, although I must have suspected that those two subjects, never mentioned more than perfunctorily, were at the heart of what I was afraid to learn. I did suspect that the reason she was uninterested in having children could be found in her childhood, but again kept quiet about my suspicion. The few times the topic came up, I settled for her flippant assessment that there were enough people in the world without us contributing to the problem.

The one affair she had, two years after we were married—no more than a few months old and for all intents and purposes over by the time I accidentally discovered it—should have opened the door for questions and answers, but I felt only relief when she gave me a matter-of-fact account of it: She had had a relationship with the man, a chemistry professor twenty-five years her senior (someone who thumbed his nose at the ethics of student/teacher relationships), before I knew her. There had been a hiatus in their contact for several years while he was out of the country doing research at Cambridge, but they had begun seeing each other again after his return. Except now it was over and done with, and Vida referred to it as a stupid infatuation with a self-important nobody. I settled for her assessment and did not press the issue. Not that I believed things to have been that simple. I recognized that for months after the breakup she missed him and was suffering, and I couldn't help but feel stabs of jealousy at seeing her emotional energy invested in him. But the attitude I cultivated was that I respected her need to come to terms with her feelings on her own. More likely, I was simply hiding from my cowardly self my fear that if I asked her, she would tell me what quality unattainable by me had drawn her to this self-important nobody, and that in telling me she would decide I was failing her and would leave me.

And yet, after all this rending of garments and conscientious self-laceration, I have not delved into that far murkier area—the motive behind the motive, which turned so much of what I did and did not do with respect to Vida into something pernicious. What is the greatest sin we commit with respect to those we love? Is it to make an image of them by saying, You are this and that, and I know you? Or is it to take this image and try to keep frozen in time the one we forced to pose for the portrait? Is the true cowardice to give in to the fear that someone we need to be this way and no other— for whatever suspect psychological reasons—may change? So we fight change by gathering herbs at midnight and placing them on a sleeping brow, and, if we succeed, harm most what we love best.

And yet again, all obscure, disreputable motives aside, and despite the conscious and unconscious distancing I practiced with respect to certain areas in Vida's life, the passing years did not diminish my feelings for her. And all irritation and annoyance and the wear and tear of daily life with her at a time when both of us—she a great deal more than I—were troubled did not change the fact that there was a place in my heart in which I was ready to love her unconditionally.

I did not suffer a relapse as a result of Sunday's sightseeing but felt listless when on Monday morning Vida and Jim headed off to their respective projects and I was left to my own devices at the villa. I had brought my manuscript and notes. But I felt uninspired when I sat down in the living room and tried to pick up where I had left off. The villa was still a strange place to me since so far I had spent most of my time there in bed. I became aware of birds chirping and aggressively upending and flinging aside wet leaves on the grass in search of grubs, the chink-chink sound of stonework being done in one of the nearby gardens; otherwise there was nothing to lull my city ears with a comforting envelope of noise. I noticed piles of papers Vida had collected on a low cupboard and I browsed through them in search of distraction.

In addition to a creditable amount of first-draft material on her distinguished subject, there were several reprints of articles by Fry, all, judging by their titles, concerned with what Fry called Coincidence Theory. I assumed they would be Greek to me, but I leafed through one of them. As I had suspected, it had a great deal of mathematical formalism. I began reading it anyway and found I understood a surprisingly large amount of what Fry was discussing because he wrote in a clear, uncluttered prose. The article was on "complex dynamical systems." It argued that the formation of patterns in seemingly random processes suggested that even though these patterns were unpredictable and irreproducible, they followed hidden laws of coincidence within themselves as if their evolution followed a drive toward "self-similarity." Fry's main example was fractals—a mathematical concept that characterized objects, such as coastlines or mountain ranges, exhibiting the same jaggedness or smoothness viewed from any distance—and once he went into details, things quickly became too mathematical for me.

Another article, this one blessedly low on equations, argued that all of the so-called psi effects—from telepathy to psychokinesis—could be explained in two ways, either of which would account for all observations of, again so-called, extrasensory perception: they could, as was done traditionally, be attributed to additional senses or mental powers, or they could be seen as the manifestation of an "acausal force" striving to create coincidences in events. "Events" in this context meant any occurrence in the physical world, from a brick falling off a roof to a random thought about someone one hadn't seen in twenty years. The psychokinetic effect of a subject "making" a die land preferentially with a particular face up could, for example, be explained equally well by the argument that the subject, in wishing for that face to be up, set the stage for that face to come up coincidentally. The same was true of telepathy: one could either postulate a mental force linking two minds or could argue that the fact that one mind thought a certain thought created the condition for another to coincidentally have the same thought. Fry, giving passing credit to a book by Arthur Koestler, titled *The Roots of Coincidence*, concluded that the observations could be explained by either theory, just as any observation concerning evolution could equally well be explained by Darwinian or Lamarckian arguments.

Yet another article was apparently work in progress since it had manual corrections and was unfinished. It had to do with precognition, and I found it to be oddly obscure compared to the others. The feeling I had was that Fry was forever trying to say what he was reluctant to say. There seemed to be a tug-of-war between his wanting to clarify something and wanting to avoid or skirt that same something. Clear enough was that he thought precognition to be connected with his conception of coincidence. According to him, previous knowledge of something that then occurred was by definition coincidental, and it was pointless to ask whether the correct interpretation was that someone thought about something, which then coincidentally indeed happened, or that an event that would happen in the future had precognitively jumped into someone's head.

I had no trouble with his basic approach, which was simply a theoretical rumination along the lines of a standard thought experiment: "If we assume this, what happens if we plug in that?" But there was a hesitancy, the lack of a clearly detectable sense of what he was leading up to. It was the sort of paper I would have marked with, "Needs a purpose statement." Fry talked about coincidence as unpredictable and uninfluenceable. Almost in the same breath, he claimed that recognition of a coincidence became a part of the coincidence: a man unrelatedly running into two old friends on the same day was one coincidence; his recognition of the coincidence was another, connected, one. But, he added, suppose a man thought of an old friend in the morning and ran into him in the afternoon (obviously one of the most frequently experienced events of this kind, as in: "I don't believe it; I though of you just this morning!")—was that enough of a coincidence to satisfy whatever "force" was at work in its quest for "correlation by affinity"? And were these types of events doomed to remain forever random in the sense that any deliberate attempt to affect coincidences or to call them into existence—in other words, any attempt at control— would fail because it would perturb and change the system and make it noncoincidental? Was the problem analogous to the impossibility of observing a quantum mechanical system without the system being perturbed and changed? Or were there ways, subtle ways, in which the experimenter might minimize his control but might nevertheless exert some influence according to which a coincidental pattern would rearrange itself—again unpredictably but possibly more in the direction of a desired outcome? The article ended with a paragraph on the kind of superstition that made people wear a certain article of clothing or jewelry, or carry a charm or other item they were convinced brought them luck, for an important occasion. Fry reinterpreted this phenomenon as the recognition of a coincidence (I won the final match when I wore these socks) and the attempt at controlling coincidence (If I wear them again, maybe the same thing will happen again).

I had to smile. My great-uncle had been notoriously superstitious, to the point of once refusing to embark on an ocean voyage he had planned for months simply because he developed a slight rash, and the last time he'd had a rash, some twenty years earlier, he had nearly drowned when a rowboat had capsized. Coincidence was alive and well.

✳

Jim came home around four. They (he, the American, and a few local lads) had poured a slab and needed to wait for it to dry, he explained his early arrival. He'd been to the supermarket on his way home, and he unpacked and put away groceries. He told me, still a stranger to the household routine, not to expect Vida for a while. I said that judging by the amount of writing and interviewing she was doing, she worked like a dray horse.

"If you ask me, she's nuts," he said. "I think Fry is infecting her."

I said, "I thought you liked him."

He shrugged. "I don't have to dislike him just because he's not playing with a full deck. All that coincidence hogwash. The way she carries on you'd think he'd invented sliced bread."

I realized that during the week I had been out of commission more had happened around me than the discovery of where the best pizza in town was to be found.

"You don't believe all that crap, do you?" Jim continued. "About patterns we don't have any control over—things just happening because there is this hokey acausal force out there wanting them to be connected?"

"Not as gospel truth," I said. "But there are more things in heaven and on earth, et cetera."

"There's also such a thing as common sense."

"That is violated in every significant aspect of modern physics."

"Yes, but we're not talking about modern physics. We're talking about good old uncomplicated life."

"Now you're joking," I said, and went back to Great-uncle Joshua.

Jim began dinner a short while later—too early, I thought, according to his own warning not to expect Vida for a while—but since it was stew, I said nothing. He also began to work on the wine and was on his third or fourth glass by the time dinner was ready. It was dark outside by the time he had finished. I cleared my things off the table, and he put out plates and silverware and said, "Well, I don't know about you, but since there's no knowing if the author will make her appearance before midnight, I'm eating."

I surmised that this was not the first time Vida had come back to the villa late and Jim had had to eat by himself, with me in bed lost to the world. I also surmised that Jim's unhappiness with the current state of affairs went deeper than disgruntledness at Vida's occasional absence at dinner. Vida had so far been too busy for their usual daily run, and with the sole exception of the energetic spear-gun practice there had been no working out together. Small wonder Jim resented being neglected.

When a few minutes later the hum of the electric gate opening announced Vida's arrival, Jim put out a third plate and silverware for her, but his mood didn't improve when she began at once telling us about a talk Fry had given at the weekly colloquium. The subject had been chaos and he had been amusing, witty, brilliant. The question-and-answer period, too, had been remarkable: Fry immediately saw what was at the core of any question, and his answers were lucid. Afterwards, she talked to one of the people who had been there. He said Geoff was uncanny: sometimes you asked him a question and you yourself weren't even sure what was bothering you, but he would instantly figure it out and not only give you the answer but explain the question to you.

I could see how her enrapturedness might get on Jim's nerves—not that it was notably lifting my own spirits—and I changed the subject by complimenting her on a turquoise, wide-necked velvet top she had bought at one of the boutiques. In fashionable Frascati, Vida made concessions to the Italians' innate sense of style by dressing stylishly instead of running around in her usual jeans and sweats. She wore black slacks and had bought, also at one of the local stores, a pair of low-heel but fashionable shoes, arguing that the panel that had given her her grant wouldn't disapprove of her spending some of the loot to represent the U.S. in style. Looking at her across the table, talking to Jim, whose bad mood had lifted, I thought that I didn't in fact like her new top—it didn't suit her. I was reminded of the children prancing about in their grown-up *carnevale* costumes—except in their case the make-believe was charming, and in hers all I could see was her affecting an annoying sophistication.

After dinner we bundled up because the nights were cold, unusually so according to the locals, and took a walk to the center of town. Despite the cold, a great many people were milling about everywhere, couples, larger groups, gatherings of teenagers. We went to the Piazza del Duomo, where the dome was a gray bulk doused in floodlights. Jim had been inside once before, but Vida and I hadn't. We entered the empty, sepulchral gloom of too few lights in too large a space. The usual gold and tinsel around the altars glinted dully, the reds were brown, the blues gray; we were alone with two people sightseeing at the other end of the church, and we spoke in the hushed, self-conscious tone of people aware of being on alien ground considered sacred. Every word came back with the hollow echo given to sound by large, stone-enclosed spaces.

Jim was the one who alerted us to the "citizens in the columns." Here and there, not only on columns but walls and the floor as well, marble plaques announced with a *Hic Requiescit* that behind or below the plaque were the remains of a former inhabitant of Frascati. The presence of the dead at eye level was nothing new to me—I had visited dozens of English churches while gathering material for my dissertation on the effect of the plagues on English social life. I read a few of the inscriptions, all in Latin, and lost interest. Jim and I began a sotto-voce discussion concerning a particularly garish piece of altar art, some saint's martyrdom, that loomed gigantically in one of the side altars. When next I looked for Vida, she had moved down the rows of columns, still studying the memorial plaques on them with a systematic interest. We joined her. "Anything riveting?" I asked.

She said, "My Latin isn't good enough."

I translated the inscription on the plaque before us: some worthy gentleman, pious, upright, honorable; beloved husband, cherished father—not of this world these hundred years according to the date of death.

"Is it sanitary to bury corpses like this?" Vida asked still in a half-whisper even though the tourists had left.

I was startled by the question.

"Isn't the air around dead bodies tainted?" she elaborated.

"Sure, but the opening was sealed airtight."

"You don't want your worshipers to attend Mass holding their noses," Jim agreed.

Vida shivered and said—no longer in a whisper but loudly as if she didn't care who might hear—"I still think it's a stupid idea." Having had her say, she turned on her heels and made for the exit.

I thought of her accusation after our visit to the Etruscan museum that I lacked imagination with respect to quaint funeral practices. Who was lacking imagination now? Before I could make an observation along those lines to Jim, he leaned towards me and said under his breath, "She wants to be cremated."

I felt disoriented, as if he had suddenly started speaking in another language and I hadn't yet made the adjustment to the new sounds. "Maybe," I said.

"No, not maybe. Definitely. She's told me so."

Vida had reached the exit and the heavy door fell shut behind her with a hollow boom. I tried to find my bearing. Vida had never discussed funeral arrangements with me, and here, in a church festooned with immured corpses, was Jim telling me what she wanted done in the event of . . . I don't know what I replied, probably, "Ah," or, "I see," while trying not to feel jealous about my wife having confided in our friend rather than me about something so intimate.

On our way back to the villa we talked about the Italian propensity for commemorating any occasion with a marble plaque. Jim had found one announcing that Garibaldi had "recovered in this house" after one of his campaigns and another one, outside a church, proclaiming the gratitude of Frascati for having been saved from a plague that had decimated a nearby village. "Your territory," he added, nudging me.

"I like that," Vida said. "Thank you, Lord, for goring the

other bloke's ox." She had apparently recovered from her moment of eschatological angst.

While Jim was unlocking the door to our apartment, I moved over to a corner and inspected the wall. "Wait a minute. What's that?" I said. "It's very faint but I can just make it out: Caius Julius Caesar slept here."

"Does it say with whom?" asked Vida.

We all laughed.

That night Vida and I made love—our first time in Italy. When I went to sleep, my last thought was that our Italian adventure would turn out fine after all.

But I woke up in the middle of the night from a dream in which a voice whispered into my ear: "She wants to be cremated." And I was gripped by mortal terror and sweated and trembled at the thought of the inevitable death of someone I loved.

A FEW DAYS LATER, VIDA BROUGHT AN INVITATION FROM
Fry: the three of us at his house for dinner, prepared by his
part-time housekeeper, who could sometimes be persuaded
to cook for *il professore*. Our host picked us up around eight
and drove us a short distance outside Frascati to a small villa
situated in an old olive grove. He told us about his landlord,
owner of a local winery, who insisted on keeping him
stocked with cases of the white wine he produced. At the
house we sampled the fare, gave it our seal of approval and
settled down to dinner—frutti di mare and polenta, neither
of which I was crazy about, but Vida, in a blue-green silky
dress for the occasion, her pale hair gathered at the top of her
head in a black velvet ribbon and spilling down her back,
rhapsodized about the blending of flavors in the fishy broth.

After dinner, when Fry was out of the room for a
moment, Jim strolled over to a baby grand piano in a corner,
sat down on the bench and pounded out a rapid jig. I hadn't

known he played the piano, and I asked him how good he was.

"Not very," he said. "Five years of wasted lessons." He looked at sheet music propped up on the piano, checked its cover and let out a whistle. "Unlike our host. Look at that: Bach's Chaconne via Busoni."

I went over to the piano and looked at line after line of complicated garlands of notes. "Difficult?" I asked.

"Try impossible. There must be fifteen pages of it. By the time you learn page five you've forgotten about pages one through four. And technically you have to be a contortionist." He scanned the page the book was open to and pointed at a spot. "That goes something like this." He played eight or nine notes slowly at first and then more rapidly, his fingers performing an involved sequence of movements on the keys.

Fry came into the room and said, "Music hath charms, et cetera."

Jim said, "I didn't think the Chaconne could be played by anyone who wasn't a concert pianist."

"You were right. I've spent the last six months practicing it, and if I live to be a thousand, all I'll ever do is practice it."

Vida said, "I'd like to hear what it sounds like. Could you practice it now?"

Fry hesitated. "As if the unlovely prospect of Bach and Busoni gyrating in their graves weren't bad enough. Well, I suppose you can always plug your ears with your fingers or run for the hills if things get too bad."

Jim got up from the bench but stayed next to it when Fry sat down. "Let's see if I still know enough to turn the pages," he said. "When did you start learning to play?"

"A deplorably short while ago. Twelve years. I desperately

needed something to get elementary particles out of my head and decided on the piano." Fry turned to the first page, placed his hands on the keys, opened his eyes unnaturally wide in looking at the sheet music before him as if he hoped to see more, and began to play. I sat down on a chair near Vida and listened. A stately procession of notes began to fill the room. Fry played well what seemed to my nonexpert ear a not-too-difficult passage. But after a few phrases, the music turned into a rapid staccato of ascending and descending notes, a complicated mixture of sounds that washed over us like a torrent. Fry's playing struck me as miraculous. His technique seemed flawless, and he gave the emerging theme gravity and fire, so that the music was at once solemn and full of a passionate appeal for abandon and transport. I was not familiar with the original work, but it occurred to me that the transcription had made Bach almost unbearably romantic.

I became aware of Fry's housekeeper, a short, solid woman, standing in the doorway, listening. I smiled at her and indicated my admiration of Fry with a nod in his direction. She turned her eyes heavenward, I wasn't sure whether in agreement or in mock exasperation at the mighty din of the piano, and returned to her kitchen chores. Jim meanwhile was following Fry with his eyes on the sheet music, turning the pages for him. Vida sat, her eyes closed, her hands folded in her lap. On her face was a look of intense concentration as if she were listening for something hidden in the music that only the most careful attention could detect. I wondered whether she felt how sad the piece had become in all its passion. Then I saw a rim of wetness form between the lids of her closed eyes and two glistening lines run down her cheeks. When Fry stopped playing suddenly at the end of a phrase, she kept her eyes closed but quickly brought up her hand and wiped its back across them.

"That's it," Fry said turning to us. "Beyond here a funereal pace is all I can manage. Talk to me in a month, I may have a few more measures by then."

"That was marvelous," I told him. "What an amazing piece of music."

"Yes," Fry said. "It's where the sublime and the gladness of living meet the tears of things—sadness and delight rolled up into one ball." He stood up suddenly and closed the piano cover. "Who's in the mood for an exotic experience?"

"Like the duke's sinister tower?" I asked.

"Rather more exotic. A mixture between a parlor game and an oracle."

"Why not?"

"Anyone else?"

Vida raised her hand.

"A silent assent," Fry said and moved to turn to Jim. But he paused and asked Vida, "Are you all right?"

She nodded and seemed about to say something, but Jim cut in. "I know. A Ouija board. Just what I always wanted for Christmas."

"No, but a relative. Wait and see."

In the car Fry told us more about the entertainment ahead. "Regarding this up-and-coming exotic experience—you may be skeptical about what you'll see and be told. If so, don't worry about it. It's an experiment of sorts, but if my theory is correct the outcome won't be biased by your reaction. I might as well tell you that what's involved is a reading, or several readings, of the tarot by what is arguably the best reader to be found in Italy. Don't look for any spectacular revelations, but if you're at all interested, listen, and you may be surprised."

We had reached the Piazza del Duomo. Slowing down to wait for milling pedestrians to get out of the way, Fry drove down narrow roads flanked by buildings to a place where the houses ended and, on the far side of a piazza, the ground fell away behind a low wall and black country lay under a sky only minutely lighter. "You get quite a view during the day or when the moon is out," Fry said.

The row of buildings facing the view had stairs leading to basement rooms. Fry led us down one of them. Through a window, we saw into a room. An elderly man sat at a table reading a newspaper. He looked up when he heard us on the stairs, folded the paper and came to the door to greet us. I had anticipated something exotic, a dark Gypsy mane, coal-black eyes, a collarless shirt. Instead Signor Enrico Valga, as Fry introduced him, had short, gray hair, gold-framed aviator glasses, and wore a wool sweater over a shirt and tie. He could have been an accountant, dentist or academic.

Valga greeted us in Italian, told us to take off our coats and put them on a table in the corner and sit anywhere at the round table. He pointed and gestured so we would have understood even if Fry hadn't translated. He closed the curtains, turned on a lamp hanging directly over the table and turned off two wall lamps. The effect was that the table and those sitting at it were in an orb of yellow light while everything else in the room was dark. Valga took a deck of cards from a drawer in the table, sat down in his chair and briefly looked at each of us. Then he pointed at me, sitting nearest to him, and said something to me. Fry translated: "Think of an area of your life that you are currently concerned about, or ask a question."

I felt odd about being picked to go first in Fry's parlor game-cum-experiment. "What, me?" I said. "I haven't a care in the world."

"Try to be serious."

I tried to think about something but drew a blank. The others looking at me made me self-conscious and I had the feeling I was on a stage complete with props and lighting. What finally jumped into my mind was the naive question: Will I be happy? "Do I have to say it out loud?" I asked Fry.

"No. Just keep it in mind."

Valga handed me the deck of cards and indicated through a shuffling motion what I was to do with it. I shuffled the cards until he said, "*Basta.*" He demonstrated with an imaginary deck that I was to cut the cards twice. I did, and he merged the three stacks in a different order. Then he pulled the first card from the top of the pack face down and turned it and placed it on the table.

Fry, sitting next to me, let out a low whistle. The card was the same he had shown me in the duke's tower: a tower shattered by lightning, two figures being hurled head over heels from it. Valga pulled the next card off the top and placed it perpendicular across the tower. It showed a man dressed in medieval garb leaning on a tall stick. Behind him a row of other sticks was planted in the ground. Valga rapidly dealt out another eight cards, four counterclockwise at the four compass points so they completed a cross, and another four in a vertical column next to the cross. Then he set the rest of the deck aside, folded his hands before his mouth and studied the spread.

I had never seen tarot cards, and I was fascinated by their colorful iconography, the wealth of symbols and attitudes of the figures. The card that first caught my attention depicted a figure sitting up in a bed and covering its face with both hands as if consumed by the deepest sorrow. Mounted horizontally behind the figure was a grid of broadswords. Another sword card showed a man holding three swords while the swords of two men in the background were lying on the ground. But two other cards, both in the vertical row, arrested my roaming eye. One garishly depicted the devil, all hair and horns and malice, seated on a throne, the chained, naked figures of a man and a woman at his feet; the other showed a young man in a short tunic and soft boots, carrying a satchel on a stick on his shoulder and a rose in his raised hand. He was light-footed, frozen in a skip or dance; his eyes were on the sky, but at his feet was a precipice and one step further would propel him over the edge of the cliff. It seemed to me that these were not happy cards and I felt the stirring of a superstitious regret at having asked, of all possible things, a question about happiness.

Valga took his hands from his mouth and began to talk in a low voice. Fry interrupted him to translate, and Valga built pauses into his reading to allow Fry to catch up.

"You are concerned with a matter in which there is grave doubt that what you wish can be achieved. If it is achieved it will be in a way you didn't suspect. You've in the past attempted to gain advantage by unethical means—no, by means others have considered unethical," Fry corrected himself, "and you have suffered a reversal of fortune. Now an even more cataclysmic change lies ahead. In this change you'll learn what you didn't know, but the knowledge will be gained at the cost of suffering, mental or physical. There is a threat of loss of what you love, but you have the resources to triumph over it. Your balance is precarious and you will have to make a vital choice. The step to a new life may require you to place yourself in a position of lack of control or even danger—in other words, nothing ventured, nothing gained, to put a more prosaic cast on things."

Valga added something and raked in the cards.

"And that's all he can see," Fry paraphrased.

Valga handed the deck to Vida. She said, "I don't know if I want to. That sounded pretty ominous."

"Courage," I told her. "What's a little threat to life, limb, or the pursuit of happiness?"

She asked Fry, "Tell me again what I'm supposed to think about."

"Something that currently interests you, troubles you, worries you; a question you may have about the future—or the past or present for that matter."

She closed her eyes and affected a frown of concentration. "Ready," she then said, and began shuffling the cards. Again Valga made her stop when he was satisfied and had her cut the deck twice. This time the first card he pulled off the top was the grieving figure beneath the wall of swords. The other cards followed in rapid succession; three more had swords being brandished or handled, a fourth displayed a heart skewered by three swords. The last card that Valga placed on the table, on top of the vertical column, showed a horseman in black armor. The helmet's visor was open and a skull grinned down on a prostrate man and woman.

None of us moved, and I felt cold creeping toward my heart from the tips of my fingers and toes. Fry was the first to speak. "This is not a card of death," he said. "It's a metaphor for transformation—a change from one state to another."

Valga shot him a sharp glance of disapproval and began his reading of the cards. Fry translated: "The subject is beset by a conflict and knows not where to turn without hurting or doing harm to herself or others. The past is dead—no, *lost* is the better word—but it clings to the present and threatens to strangle it. There may be danger to one you love. There may be perils, deception, secret foes. The difficulties are grave—I'm sorry this is turning into gloom and doom—ah, but a champion rides with you, and there are also hidden forces for good at work. The result may be a transformation for the better."

Jim, who had been silent throughout, suddenly spoke up. "What does the nine of swords stand for?" He pointed at the grieving figure beneath the grid of swords.

"Desolation, doubt, suffering, death—not of the subject but someone near the subject. Any or all of the above."

Vida kept her eyes on the cards and remained silent. I wondered whether she, too, regretted the question she had asked the tarot.

Valga said something and collected the cards.

"That's all I can see," Fry translated literally. He added in an aside, "He does like to be emphatic about the limitations of his abilities. You're next, Jim. Shuffle and see what the cards have to say."

Valga extended the deck to Jim, but Jim raised his hands palms out and said, "No thanks, I pass."

Valga gave Fry a questioning look, and Fry, not taking his eyes off Jim, said with a distracted frown, "*Non vuole,*" which was close enough to Latin for me to translate as, He doesn't want to.

Valga theatrically pulled up his shoulders and began to shuffle the deck.

Jim asked, "*Che fa?*" and when Valga ignored him: "What's he up to now?"

"He'll make do without your help. There is no real need for the subject to shuffle the cards if the reader has a sense of him. Apparently he has a sense of you."

Valga put down the deck and cut it twice, then reunited the three stacks. He turned over the first card and gently put it on the table. It was the young man frozen in his skipping dance at the edge of the chasm.

"*Il Matto,*" Fry said. "The Fool at the precipice. A vital choice to be made—wisely for good, foolishly for ill."

Jim was suddenly on his feet. "I don't want him to do it. *Basta,*" he said to Valga. "*Non voglio. Basta!*"

Valga looked at Fry, the hand holding the second card suspended in midair. Fry shook his head and said something in rapid Italian. Then he said to Jim, "I had no idea you were a believer."

"I'm not, but I don't like anybody acting as if he knew things about me that I don't know—and I'm supposed to pretend I'm being told some great secret."

Valga smiled and crossed the young man with the next card. It depicted an unclad young woman kneeling on one knee and pouring water from two pitchers, one onto grass at her side, the other into a pool of water on which her forward foot was resting. Overhead a large yellow star, surrounded by several smaller white stars, lit up the sky. *Le Stelle*, the words on the card said.

Fry pointed at it. "At any rate, your fear may be unfounded. The Star means that unselfish aid will be given."

But Jim turned without saying another word and was out the door. We heard him on the stairs, then all was quiet.

Fry said. "I'm sorry. I had no idea he was serious. I better go after him and apologize." He quickly said something to Valga and we all left after collecting our coats.

Jim was standing at the viewpoint, looking out over the black country.

Handing him his coat, Fry said, "I'm sorry. I didn't mean to upset you."

Jim thanked him and put on his coat. "I never could stand fortune tellers," he said. "Not even at county fairs. They gave me the creeps."

"We all have our pet willies," Fry sympathized. "I hope all of this hasn't been too depressing. There are bound to be times when the trouble-and-strife cards dominate. No point losing sleep over it." He checked his watch. "Five minutes to get you home before the stroke of midnight."

During the drive a question occurred to me. "Did your experiment at the tower also have something to do with the tarot?" I asked Fry.

He laughed and said, "Very little." Then he checked himself. "Oh, you mean the one I did months ago; the one with all the hardware. Yes. I was looking for one of Kammerer's correlations by affinity—you remember Kammerer, the unlucky biologist with the ruined career and the coincidence fixation? Will a tarot deck used inside a calamitous tower burp up a predominance of tower cards? The actual question

I asked is more complicated, but I don't want to induce terminal boredom."

"You mean you kept spreading the cards to see how many towers there'd be compared to how many you got elsewhere?" I asked.

"As I said, it's more complicated. And I did only a small part of it manually and had Valga do another small part. Mainly, I wrote a program that simulated the process of shuffling, spreading and reading the cards. I had to build a white-noise random-numbers generator in order to get truly random shuffling. And I ran it for a few weeks to get a large sampling."

"And?"

"The result was statistically significant, five percent more hits than I got running the same program at the lab."

"Meaning what? That where the cards are is more important than what they say about the subject?"

"Meaning that there is a correlation by affinity, and that on some level that correlation can be created."

We had arrived at the gate to the villa, and we got out of the car and thanked Fry for dinner and the evening's entertainment. He laughed and said, "Unselfish aid will be given. Good night to you all."

We took the usual turns in the bathroom to get ready for bed: first Vida, then me, then Jim. In bed, with the lights out, I asked Vida, "What was your question to the oracle?"

She gave a loud yawn. "Nothing earthshaking: Will I finish my book by the end of the year?"

She did not ask me about my question, and I was glad

because this seemed to me neither the time nor place to tell her that I was not happy, and how much of my not being happy had to do with her.

An hour later I was still wide awake, listening to Vida's quiet breathing and feeling afraid. Jim, young, hale and hearty Jim, had been afraid of the cards, and I was afraid now—of what the cards had hinted at, of the future, change, loss of what I loved. I tried to tell myself that what I had seen had been a parlor game, no more. Yes, there had been the occasional disconcerting correlation with life, but what was not correlated in this world? What random jumble of concepts or words would not tell an uncannily connected story if presented linearly?

But all the time the cards appeared more and more vividly before my inner eye. The broken tower with its figures hurtling toward destruction. The reckless boy, The Fool according to Fry, on the brink of the abyss—the meaning a choice of vital importance to be made. Death the black horseman—the meaning not death but transformation, a change from one state to another—only I didn't believe Fry and saw that grinning horseman in the last line of an otherwise forgotten nursery rhyme as "Death, and Death, and Death indeed."

I got up, got dressed in the dark and left the villa. With no clear idea of where I was heading, I walked rapidly through the deserted roads, up to the dome. Once there, I knew my destination. I found the way, down narrow lanes, the last ending at the viewpoint and Signor Valga's home.

Fry's car was back, parked at the same spot. Why I wasn't surprised to see it there I don't know. I gingerly approached the stairs leading to Valga's door. There was a crack in the heavy curtain. I peered through it and saw Valga sitting at the table looking motionless at a spread of cards before him. Or almost motionless: the gold frames of his glasses glinted off and on while he was almost imperceptibly nodding as if he were mentally counting. Fry was sitting opposite him; all I saw was the back of his balding head and a fraction—a sliver of cheek, the hint of an eye—of his face. He was watching Valga with intense, unwavering concentration. In the orb of yellow light thrown on the scene by the overhead lamp, the two figures looked like a painting by one of the Flemish masters. I knew the title: *The Soothsayer and His Client*. In the painting, the cards on the table would not be discernible, just as they weren't discernible by me, but by a trick in perspective used by the painter, the spectator would be able to identify them by looking at them from an extreme angle or in a distorting mirror.

Suddenly Valga began to talk. No sound penetrated the window, and I had the feeling of watching a scene taking place elsewhere—as unperturbed and unperturbable by my presence as images on a movie screen. Valga pointed at one card, then another, stabbed at yet another with an accusing index finger. Fry shook his head, nodded, talked agitatedly, pointed at cards. Valga leaned back, took off his glasses and pulled a handkerchief from his pocket. He cleaned his glasses, put them back on, leaned forward and looked at the cards again as if in the hope of seeing more. He shook his head and began to push the cards around in a circular motion as if he were stirring a broth, then collected and shuffled them. He seemed ready to lay out the cards again when Fry rose abruptly and pulled out his wallet.

Things suddenly became real enough. I was afraid of being

caught spying and quickly made my way up the stairs and over to the balustrade overlooking the town and dark country. Moments later, Fry came out, saying *"Buona notte"* to Valga. He walked to his car, but noticing me, he called, "Hello. Why aren't you in bed sleeping the sleep of the just?" and strolled over to me.

"I couldn't sleep," I said. "So I wandered through the town like a damned soul and promptly got lost until I found this place."

"I was afraid Enrico's feathers might have been a tad ruffled by our Mr. Quarrel's refusal to be enlightened. So I came back to soothe them. Then he started telling me about the war—he was an eighteen-year-old gunner at Anzio—and I couldn't leave." Fry stood next to me and we both looked out over the black countryside. "From Caesar's legions to American infantry, this place has seen it all," Fry commented.

"And has it learned anything from what it has seen?"

"I should think not." Uttering a dramatic "Brrr," Fry buttoned up his leather coat. "What about you? Are you learning anything?" he asked.

"You mean besides not trusting the tarot?"

He looked at me from the side. "One useful thing about the tarot is that it doesn't care whether the subject is a believer or disbeliever."

"You mean if it predicts your imminent demise you'll die whether or not you believe it?"

"That's overstating things. Nobody has the skill to read that kind of change from the cards."

"But Valga read that one of us is going to die." My statement came out of nowhere. Having made it, I felt thunderstruck.

Fry's hand was suddenly on my elbow and he held my arm with a vise grip. "What on earth made you say that?" he asked. "Do you have the slightest idea what you're talking about?"

I said, "No, I don't. I don't know what made me say that. Sleep deprivation probably. Or a momentary compulsion to be dramatic. Maybe it was a feeble attempt at humor. I don't know."

He let go of my arm. "This place gives me the creeps, to use Jim's expression," he said, and without transition continued, "All Valga really told you, once you ignore the alarming picture show, was that there are difficulties ahead—possibly connected with someone you care about. Interestingly, he told Vida the same thing."

"Which argues we are each other's respective difficulties."

"Unless either or both of you don't care about the other."

"We do—even if it ain't always obvious."

Fry let out a short laugh. "No doubt. As for the redoubtable Mr. Quarrel, there is nothing sinister in what Valga would have told him, a vital choice to be made, an important change ahead, a warning against false friends— not you or Vida, I'm sure." He caught my askance look. "Yes, I had Valga do a reading in absentia. Sheer perversity on my part. I hope you're not scandalized."

"How could I be? I'm not a believer. Anyway, it seems to me any halfway-decent fortune teller will tell you all you know about yourself and what's going on in your life."

To my surprise Fry agreed, "Yes, either by recognizing subtle clues or by turning himself into a receptacle for coincidence—let's say the subject happens to be a gambler and thoughts of gambling jump coincidentally into the mind of the fortune teller. Or, in the case of the tarot, by the cards coincidentally being arranged by the shuffling in such a way as to reflect things going on in your life."

"Maybe. But a lot of it has to be just formula. Don't tell me the meanings of the cards aren't vague enough to provide generic insights. 'You're having difficulties in an area of your life; you've suffered a reversal of fortune from which recovery is slow,' et cetera, et cetera. As in who hasn't?"

Fry pondered my question, then said abruptly, "Why were you denied tenure?"

My first impulse was to tell him that my life was none of his business. But the night had been strange from the beginning and there was something fitting to my telling the story of my reversal of fortune now. I told Fry with a matter-of-factness that amazed me about my tenure book, a comprehensive look at how the bubonic plague had affected social life in England between 1665 and 1900. I had collected a wealth of data during a four-month trip to England while I was in graduate school and during one summer when I was a tenure-track assistant professor. In writing my book I drew on bills of mortality, parish and churchyard records, reports of medical examiners, announcements of quarantines, closed schools, postponed theatrical events and concerts, private letters talking of changes in household routines, and so forth. The information was in reams of notes and copies of documents. In addition I had checked out a hundred and fifty or so books from the library. After a final six-month push that took every ounce of my organizational ability and dogged determination, I submitted "All Fall Down: The Social Impact of the Black Death from 1665 to 1900" to a renowned university press. Three months later it was accepted for publication. I added the letter of acceptance to the manuscript I had given to the tenure committee and sat back in the sure and certain knowledge that my associateship was a done deal.

Then the freakish thing happened. One of my esteemed colleagues, who had been in England the summer before, doing research on High-Church intrigues in the nineteenth century, remembered learning that all the records of a certain London suburb had been destroyed in a fire during a bombing raid in 1940. Yet figures from these records were in my book. He made discreet inquiries to make sure his memory didn't fail him and began to dig. Through what must have been no small effort on his part, he located the out-of-print 1901 book containing the numbers that had gone up in smoke forty years later—a *clearly* plagiarized secondary source since I attributed my numbers to the original records. Confronted with the accusation, I protested that I had obviously made the simple mistake of losing track amid the paper blizzard of where a few sheets of figures had come from; nothing would have been easier than to cite the proper source. But my nemesis was ready. He had, laborious mole, found a paragraph in my book (an entire paragraph in a book of some one thousand paragraphs) that existed virtually verbatim in another out-of-print book, this one published in 1972. And, yes, it was among the books I had checked out of the library. Case closed. End of academic career.

How that paragraph had found its way into my text I didn't know. With the exception of one short section, the one containing the land-mine paragraph, the "plagiarized" book treated topics far from my area of interest; I didn't remember ever even opening it. I once asked a mathematician what the probability was of someone by pure chance writing a paragraph that someone else had written. He said it obviously depended on length and complexity, but for something of the length and complexity I described the answer was close to zero. "You'd disagree, though, wouldn't you?" I asked Fry. "It fits your theory of coincidence."

He said, "Yes, I would have been your champion. I would have pointed out that your paragraph is a totally unbelievable coincidence, the likes of which can be found a million times a day by anyone who looks for it. Of course it's also possible that you did read that section of the book, subconsciously committed it to memory, and remembered it without knowing you were remembering it when it came in handy. Or even that you did copy it from the book and repressed the memory of having done so. In any event, it's a rotten thing to have had your career destroyed by something so minor."

I was surprised at the note of genuine sympathy in his voice. I said, "I had fantasies of killing my dear colleague in some fiendishly ingenious way for more than a year. That and burning the university and all its learned papers to the ground. But it passed. Anyway, worse things have happened to people, and worse things will happen to me."

Fry had put his hands in his pockets. He shivered and I wondered why he didn't suggest we get out of the cold. "What makes you say that?" he asked.

"I was speaking generally. Everybody dies in the end, 'everybody' includes me; therefore I'll die in the end."

Fry laughed. "*Moro, ergo sum.* But who knows when that end may be—tonight? in thirty years?"

"Ask Signor Valga." I thought I had made a joke, but Fry took the statement seriously.

"He can't tell. He can tell you a lot of things, but they are

97

probabilities rather than facts. The probability may be so high that it approaches certainty, but it will never be certainty until the future encounters the present. That's what gives predictions of the future usefulness beyond that of, say, allowing you to get your affairs in order before you depart from this vale of tears. If the future were absolute certainty, you might as well just sit still and wait for what you know will happen to happen."

"As opposed to doing what? If it will happen in the future, then isn't there by definition nothing you can do about it?"

"You're not listening. I said the future is a probability, not a certainty. Suppose I were to find out that there is a high probability I'll be killed in a plane crash. I can lower that probability drastically by not traveling in an airplane."

"But then the prediction would have been wrong in the first place because if you don't get into an airplane you can't crash in one."

"That's back to the old time-travel paradox: If you change the present in order to change something you see in the future, in other words, if you make a change based on information you acquire about the future, you're destroying the future's ability to furnish you with that information. Ergo you have no reason to make the change. I'm referring to something quite different. Or maybe *alluding* would be the better word since I don't seem to be able to make my point." Fry seemed bored, and I wondered why he didn't decide to call it a night. But he kept looking out at the dark country. I was about to suggest we go home and get some sleep when he continued, "A year ago I was in an accident on the *autostrada*. One of those truly freakish things. I was passing a car, and an empty shopping bag flew into the other driver's window. He jerked the steering wheel, ran me off the road, his car flipped over and he was dead on the spot. I was banged around pretty badly and ended up in the hospital with a blood clot on the brain. I nearly died during the operation. I had no vital signs for two and a half minutes. And during those two and a half minutes, I was in a place I never again want to be in." Fry paused and repeated in a flat, unemotional tone, "Never," as if stating a fact that might otherwise be missed. He paused again. "I haven't told this to anyone, but maybe this is the time for it. The place I was in during those minutes was dark, darker than the deepest night. Like I imagine it to be dark in a coffin six feet underground. 'Darkness visible,' isn't that what Milton calls it? I was there and I was aware of myself, but not as a physical entity, with arms and legs that I could move or tense, or with a face or tongue or voice. I was simply there. But I wasn't alone. There were others around me. I couldn't hear them or feel them move, but I knew they were there because I sensed them in another way. Something came from them, something I'd known only in a diluted form—and believe me, it was dreadful even in a highly diluted form. What surrounded them, and what I sensed, was pure, unrelieved, unalterable despair. All of them were in utter despair, and I knew they'd be in this state forever because there was no motion or sound or light, which meant that there was no time—so nothing could ever change. And I was one of them, encased forever in this horror with nothing to distract me from it ever, not for one moment, because I was dead."

Fry shivered. "Damn, it's cold. And now that I've made this supreme effort at the confessional I see that I'm lousy at describing what happened to me when I was dead. It seems like your run-of-the-mill nightmare, induced by too much stress, or too late a meal, or whatever. But, believe me, John, I haven't forgotten. I remember, and I know I never again want to go back there."

I thought of the obvious thing to say—that what he had experienced was a mental state caused by a momentary chemical imbalance in his brain; he might as well have felt the euphoria or sense of calm and seen the brightness at the end of a tunnel that other people have reported as near-death experiences. But that would have meant to trivialize something that was troubling him deeply. I said, "You don't believe in hell, do you?"

He said, "Don't I? I suppose I don't, since I don't believe in the opposite. I don't think what I saw was hell. I think it was something much worse. I saw what it's like to be dead and never again alive."

I protested, "But you can't possibly think . . ."

He interrupted me, "The funny thing is that there was a time in my childhood when I was absolutely horrified of death, but in quite a different way and for a different reason. When I was eight or nine I dug a hole on my grandparents' property, looking for treasure. I'd read a book that claimed there were thousands of buried caches of gold and jewelry and other valuables stashed away by people who then died or forgot where they hid them. The book also had instructions on where to look—a peculiar tree, or a large boulder, or a place where you could see two landmarks at different lines of sight. I dug at the base of an old oak. About three feet down I came across a large bone, about a foot and a half long. I thought it might belong to an extinct animal. So I dug it out and lugged it back to the house. My grandmother took one look at it and carted it off to her M.D. He identified it as a human femur. The next day policemen dug up the rest of the skeleton. It belonged to a man in his mid-fifties who'd been dead about forty years. His skull had been split, probably with an ax. There was an investigation but nothing ever came of it. The people who had owned the place back then had died, no record of a missing man fitting the description was found, and there was nothing to be done but shovel the dirt back into the hole.

"But for me it didn't end there. I couldn't get rid of the memory of having held that femur in my hands. I kept remembering the heavy, grimy feel of it and kept thinking that it had been inside the thigh of a man, with blood and flesh and muscle around it, and then he'd died and everything around it had become putrid and had dissolved. Bone has pores, and I kept thinking that the grime around that thighbone and in those pores was not all dirt but leftover decomposed flesh, and that's what I'd gotten on my hands. I washed my hands over and over and dug under my nails until I bled, but I couldn't get them clean; I knew that if I sniffed at them I'd smell the decay. So I tried never to inhale when I brought my hand close to my face when I ate, and I held my breath when washing my face.

"But the nights were the worst thing. They were appalling. Because, you see, in the night I knew, the way you never know during the day, that the time would come when I'd be a stinking skeleton. There was no way out of it. First I'd be a decomposing corpse and then bones sodden with rot. This would happen to me. Not maybe, not probably, but certainly. Night after night I lay in my bed in an icy sweat, listening to my pounding heart and horribly scared—so scared I couldn't breathe sometimes. Sometimes I thought I wouldn't live to see the light of day. I'd be a rotting corpse before the sun came up." Fry gave a deliberate dramatic shiver and turned to me. "Talk about a pleasant conversation at three in the morning. Let me take you home before you catch your death—not to change the subject or anything."

"How long did it take you to recover?" I asked, following him to the car.

"I don't know—maybe a year. There was no abrupt end. My nights of mortal terror just became fewer. I suppose the mind gets bored even of terror after a long enough time."

We drove through the dark town meeting no one. I thought about the terror of my own childhood, the years of nights when death was chasing me in my dreams, and I kept silent until we stopped at the gate of the villa. Then I thanked Fry for the ride and got out of the car. But before I could close the door, I was surprised to see him lean over and extend his hand to shake mine. I took it, a cool, dry hand.

"Good night, John," he said. "Sorry about the uninvited preview of coming attractions. Keep the goblins from ye while ye sleep."

"From you, too," I replied and shut the car door.

He laughed. "Not bloody likely!" he shouted to make himself heard, put the car in gear and drove off, up the narrow, cobbled road.

5

AND SO I STUMBLED ON, KNOWING NOTHING, ATTRIBUTING shivers and glimpses of something uncanny, and even moments of cold dread, to a general sense of disconnectedness having to do with my strange surroundings, different routine, aftermath of illness. This feeling extended to people as well. When I was with Vida or Jim or Fry—my only "contacts" during those days—I forever felt as if I were on a stage with other players, performing in some odd improvisational play. They had a script of their own lines, but it didn't tell them what anyone else on that stage would say or do; all it cued them on was roughly when to say their lines, or walk off the stage, or lash out at another player. But my own role was even more ill defined. I was without a script. Every once in a while one of the other actors would turn to me, say something, and look at me expectantly. And I'd quickly improvise a response, which was never quite satisfactory but did prompt whoever it was to turn away and continue with the scene.

If I had a suspicion that all was not well with Vida, a suspicion was all it was. Even that must have been pushed aside once jealousy entered the picture and did what jealousy does best—blind us to anything more complicated than evidence that person A is interested in person B. And just in case it wasn't difficult enough to see Vida through that distorting lens of hurt feelings and resentment, I hid my jealousy from myself by converting it into the patronizing, take-the-long-view question of just how badly she had fallen for Fry and just how long she would pine for him after our return to New York.

Still, it seems surpassingly strange to me now that I had no idea of how desperately not well things were with Vida. The greatest marvel of the entire marvelous adventure of those weeks must be how she managed to function, and give the appearance of being in control, under pressure so enormous it threatened to break her apart at any moment. Even after I remind myself that she was a master—with more than fifteen years of training—at deceiving herself and others, I find it difficult to believe how little her inner state was reflected in her behavior. I do ask myself now what would have happened if I had at any time during those weeks taken her by the elbows and shaken her and said, "What in God's name is going on inside you?" Would she have been able to tell me? Would she have told me? And would her telling me have changed the future in any significant way?

A few days after the tarot readings, Fry had to be in Rome on private business, and Vida and I were, for the first time, alone in the villa. Since the sole table was small, I did not establish my usual paper clutter on it but left room for her. She sat down opposite me and read and edited some of her notes, then read a section of an article, then hunted for another article and glanced through it. She seemed distracted, but I tried to keep my mind on my work and didn't comment. Suddenly, without lifting her head from the article, she asked: "Are you enjoying yourself?"

When I didn't answer right away, she looked up. "I mean, do you like being here?"

I said, "Sure. It's a change from the routine. How about you? Are you enjoying yourself?"

She hesitated, then said, "Yes. It's a lot of work, but yes." She seemed ready to say more but changed her mind and returned to her article. A little while later, she organized her papers and told me she had to go to the library at the Institute to look up a few things before Geoff came back the next day.

I had hoped she'd spend the day at the villa. Disappointment nettled me. "Of course. Time's a-wasting. No point spending precious hours in this dump."

She said, "I'm sorry. I know I'm always running off. But I really have to get as much as possible done while I have Geoff. Anything I don't find out now will be much harder to track down once I'm back in New York." Putting folders in her briefcase, she kept explaining why these days of proximity to Geoff were precious. I was tempted to ask her whether she really didn't know that the pull of Fry was so strong that she had to find a justification to be at least symbolically near him by spending the day at the Institute. But I hid my vexation. There was, after all, the slim chance that she herself didn't yet know she was in love with Fry. I told her that she was preaching to the converted: I certainly knew the importance of fieldwork. She left after asking me whether I'd be all right, and when I said, yes, fine, giving me a kiss on the cheek and promising she'd be back earlier than usual.

After she had left I felt keenly alone, and I remembered a time when I had felt just as alone and had been terrified of losing Vida. Three days after our arrival at the Dominican Republic, where we had planned to spend our honeymoon, Vida was in a hospital with a thirty percent chance of recovery after an operation that had removed ten inches of her intestine. She had contracted a rare amoebic parasite, and the disease was eating her alive from the inside.

She was in a small, whitewashed room looking out on a courtyard with a babbling fountain surrounded by flower beds. The little square was active from morning to night. Hurrying figures in white crossed it diagonally, patients shuffled around its perimeter, and an ancient gardener was forever pruning and puttering. The color and movement framed by the window mocked the stillness and austerity of the room and the unresponsiveness of the figure in the narrow bed.

I stayed with her day after day, did not sleep, existed on coffee and tacos, held her hand, wiped her forehead, whispered endearments, told her funny stories, recited sonnets, snatches of rhyme, nonsense—never seeing the minutest sign that she was aware of me. In a haze around me floated people in white suits; sometimes they sent me out of the room so I wouldn't see them do awful things to my wife. Sometimes they told me to sleep, told me there was nothing I could do, anything that could be done was being done. But

I knew that if I fell asleep, I would awake to the news of Vida's death.

So I held her hand, studied her face for a glimmer of recognition, wiped the corners of her mouth, said to her softly, "Sing, heigh ho, the holly! This life is most jolly," and "There is a Lady sweet and kind, Was never face so pleased my mind, I did but see her passing by, And yet I love her till I die."

But on the third day of my vigil I ran out of tales and songs, and I saw that she was dying. There was a transparency to her face, a bluish tinge I hadn't seen before. Her skin was dry and stretched over her cheekbones. I was afraid. I couldn't breathe and there was a trembling in my stomach. A nurse told me she was going to fetch a priest. I shouted at her to keep away those black vultures.

She left, and I knew I was watching Vida die and that by night I'd be more alone than I'd ever been in my life. There was a tiny pulsing in her throat. I thought, This is a promise I'm making to whoever is listening: If she lives I'll love her unconditionally, no matter what happens between us. I'll love her till I die.

A doctor came into the room, drew back one of Vida's eyelids and shone a penlight into her unfocused eye. He turned to me and said, "It is very bad."

But sometime in the middle of the night, Vida sharply drew in her breath and opened her eyes. I bent over her, and she said, "I feel awful. Have I been here long?"

Three months later she was fully recovered, running in the park, playing handball with friends, talking wryly of our honeymoon as an ordeal survived.

I never told her about the promise I had made in order to

save her, but I tried to honor it, and did, I hope, honor it as much as I was able to.

Despite the odd feeling of disconnectedness I had battled since my first day in Frascati, I had not been struck deaf and blind with respect to the third musketeer. As the days passed, I became aware that I was seeing a part of Jim I had in the past caught only a glimpse of here and there. His building project ended, and after a Sunday on which the three of us took a train to Pompeii and strolled morosely and perfunctorily through ruins that seemed flattened by brooding clouds, he hung around the villa. So as not to bother me, he bought an extension to the cable and moved the TV set into his room and watched TV by the hour. He also rediscovered the spear gun and did nothing one afternoon but shoot the lone spear into a cardboard box, trot across the lawn to retrieve it, and shoot it again. The unpredictable, resonant *thunk* when he struck the target got on my nerves, but his diverting himself outside was preferable to his moping inside.

Then he took to hiking about the countryside, lonely as a cloud. He returned in the evening, tired and terse, and rarely gave me more than a bare-essentials account of the sights he had seen. When Vida appeared around six or seven, he listened with ill-disguised boredom to her enthusiastic reports about a particularly interesting observation she had made in the company of Fry. I, too, found her frothiness excessive and understood why Jim felt left out when during dinner the only interest she showed in anything other than her own affairs appeared in obligatory questions about my progress with Great-uncle Joshua. I tried to bring Jim into the conversation by mentioning what little he had told me about his day's excursion and asking for further details about the ruined farmhouse or piece of Roman aqueduct, or whatever, he had discovered. But he invariably shrugged and said it wasn't that interesting or impressive, and he relapsed into a surly silence, which Vida ebulliently ignored.

Fry had meanwhile arranged for Vida to have a car, an impossibly small Fiat, and she drove it on the few days when it was raining, and once or twice when Fry had planned something that would keep her out until nine or ten. We used the car the Sunday after our sightseeing trip to Pompeii to drive to Tusculum, Cicero's refuge from madding Rome when he wrote his major works. Jim had spent a day hiking there and back and had reported on the ruin of a Roman amphitheater on a hill overlooking the country. Frascatians used it as a picnic spot. A lingering misguided notion of acting like people on a holiday made us pack a lunch, throw a blanket in the car and drive there.

The outing was not a success. Before we even got going, Vida and Jim squabbled over what to bring. On the way, Jim ccused Vida of copying Fry—who had taken lessons from the local lunatics—in driving like a maniac, and she slowed to a crawl, which made the local lunatics pass us with reckless abandon on blind curves. Vida's comment: "I feel so much safer, don't you?" did not contribute to domestic harmony.

At Tusculum a cold wind whipping over the barren hill forced us to cling to sandwich bags, cups, blanket, and we had no sooner settled down at a relatively sheltered spot low in the amphitheater when sheets of rain began to come down. We ran to the car but got soaked anyway and drove back wet and foul tempered. It did occur to me on the way back that this disastrous excursion could have been comical if we liked each other a little more these days, and I said something to the effect that the only reason we weren't enjoying ourselves was that we were in a bad mood.

Jim, sitting sideways in the backseat to accommodate his legs said, "Brilliant. 'If we were all happy, we'd all be happy.' Write that down."

Vida said, "Don't be a jerk."

"Which one of us?" I asked.

She didn't answer but shifted down and passed a small truck loaded with produce, and adroitly swung back into the right lane, out of the way of an oncoming car.

"I feel so much safer," said Jim.

I suppose I knew that Jim was suffering. I knew it without being consciously aware of it, thinking about it, asking myself why he was suffering, and what, if anything, I could do about it. I certainly noticed that he was drinking more. After returning from his hikes in the country, the first thing he'd do after flinging his knapsack on the couch was reach for a bottle of wine and a glass, and he'd down the first glass as if he were quenching thirst. Fry had sent via Vida a case of his landlord's vintage, so the supply was plentiful, but Jim had also bought several bottles of hard liquor, and after a few glasses of wine would switch to bourbon on the rocks.

Initially, my unexamined assumption was that what I was

seeing was the effect of boredom, and I was surprised that Jim's resources were so limited. Without a job or someone like Vida to keep him company, he was apparently lost. I couldn't help but congratulate myself on my clear advantage as the scholar perennially occupied with projects and books, and capable of taking the long view and maintaining a sanguine temper even under trying circumstances (which included a wife momentarily unhinged over another man). But as the days passed, I realized that his reaction to Vida and Fry was more than that of a neglected friend, and that poor Jim, suspecting her in love with Fry, had been infected and had fallen in love with her. Or—the thought occurred to me—maybe he had had a latent inclination for her all along and the current setup had made it flare up: never underestimate the human heart's propensity for finding the path to gratuitous hurt. Since I had every right to be more pained by Vida and Fry than he, I couldn't rouse more than a patronizing sympathy for his plight. A few days after Tusculum, my smugness got its just deserts.

I had spent the day consulting maps of Peru, Great-uncle Joshua's haunt for many years, at a library in Rome, and I returned around eight. I found Jim sitting at the table, staring into a glass while jiggling ice in it. At his elbow stood a half-empty bottle of whiskey and he was drunk.

"Howdy pardner, how's Dodge City?" he greeted me. "The Pope still wearing dresses?"

I said, "Looks like you got a head start," and I got a glass and poured myself a drink.

"Never before the stroke of noon," he said.

I asked where Vida was.

"Emergency dinner engagement with Geoff and some of

the other *testi di uova*—that's *eggheads* in my translation." He enunciated his syllables with care. "It's nice, isn't it—*testi di uova?*"

I clinked my glass against his, took a few sips and said, "So we're drowning our sorrow at the absence of our ladylove."

He looked at me from the side with red eyes hooded by thick lids and said, "You don't know shit about her, you know that?"

I contemplated his accusation. "Probably," I said. "But then who knows anything about anybody?"

"I do. I know things about her, things you don't know a fucking thing about." He flung the challenge at me and waited for my reaction.

I considered what he had said. "How do you know I don't know?" I asked.

"Because she told me." He was triumphant. "She said she's never told this to anyone. How she grew up. What happened to her."

"I know what happened to her."

"What, that she was sexually molested?" His voice gave ironic quotation marks to "sexually molested."

"Yes."

"Did she tell you how? How often? Who he was? What it felt like? Did she?"

I became aware of a sharp pain beneath my sternum and I finished my drink and poured myself another. "He was her father's adviser. She doesn't like to talk about it."

"Not to you. How could she? You're a fucking professor!"

"Ex-fucking professor."

"How could she talk to you about that and then sleep with you? Me she could tell because she knew she'd never get naked with me. And I understood her. She knew you wouldn't have understood her. Not in a million years."

"But you understand her because you love her, is that it?"

"Yes, that's it." He glared at me.

"Whereas I don't, is that right?"

"I don't know. Maybe you do. But not the way I do. I accept the fact that's she's all screwed up. I try to help her. You haven't even figured out that she's screwed up and needs help. Do you know what that bastard did to her? Her daddy's boss and adviser? Except she wasn't Vida then. She was Jenny. You didn't know that, did you? She made sure you never saw her birth certificate or found out about the name change. Jenny Eckerman, daughter of David Eckerman—original loser, and a yellow stripe this wide down his back. That's a nice name, isn't it, little Jenny Eckerman? But she hated her father so much she had to change it."

I felt I was standing at a chasm with no option but to step off the edge. To step off the edge meant to listen to Jim tell me about Vida, whom I loved, and I sat and heard what had happened fifteen years earlier to a small thin girl with tan limbs and a pageboy haircut. A child who had looked for a friend and found the devil.

✳

She met the professor when her father, a Ph.D. student working under his supervision, had him over for dinner. The professor immediately took a liking to the shy but clever girl, played a game of chess with her after dinner, drew her out of herself. He told the parents that he wished he had brought his camera. He was doing a series of photos of people, a bold step away from the landscapes he was used to doing, but he had few shots of children. Photography was currently a hobby bordering on a passion with him, and Jenny would have made a wonderful addition to his collection. But, it occurred to him, maybe she could one of these days come to his house after school. That would be more sensible anyway because all his equipment was there.

David—who wanted very much to be liked by a man of vital importance to his professional life and knew he wasn't the brightest star in the scientific firmament—was delighted. The mother had mental problems. She was at times desperately dependent on her husband, at other times withdrawn from him and the rest of the world. She agreed as a matter of course to the photo sessions.

So Jenny was photographed—standing, sitting, riding her bicycle, kicking a soccer ball, lying under a tree—smiling, pensive, dreamy, laughing, grimacing. And two of her photos appeared in a book, a collection of landscapes and portraits that netted praise for the amateur photographer.

But her visits were not all work. After each session there was chess, or the professor would read something to his subject, or they would talk. Jenny was bright and could entertain a grown man with her observations. He was a good listener and, unlike her father, forever buried in his research, or her mother, forever buried in herself, he took what she said seriously and responded to it thoughtfully. She felt she could talk to him about anything. She was an avid reader, and he lent her books, and she reported to him on what she'd read. She liked his airy study with its bay windows and glowing Persian rug and books everywhere, and she loved a grove in the back of his house, sheltered by an ivy-covered stone wall. It was overgrown with trees and shrubs, had flagstone paths covered with moss, and a tinkling fountain—a nymph pouring water from a pitcher into a pool covered with algae.

There were always a few more photos to be taken, but on many of her weekly visits, the session before the camera was short and there was more teaching than posing. Nudity in art was one interesting topic, and the professor, whom she called by then by his childhood nickname, Bliss (their secret), showed her books of studies on the female and male form in painting, sculpture and photography. He told her how important it had been for Leonardo da Vinci and Michelangelo to know what people looked like under their robes, or else they would never have achieved the right flow of fabric or angle of an arm or thigh.

Meanwhile, gradually, in the course of a year, Bliss let his little friend get closer to him. First there were hello and goodbye hugs, then kisses on the cheek. He had a beard, and she joked about the tickle until they switched to affectionate kisses on the mouth.

None of which she told her parents.

Then Bliss acquired costumes for Jenny for a new series of photos, and she posed for him in his study dressed up as a young prince in hose, doublet, pantaloons, buckled shoes, one hand on the hilt of a short dagger. Or she stood in his grove, a young Artemis leaning on a spear, one budding breast exposed, or was a child of the jungle in leopard-spotted loincloth, her young chest bare. During their last summer, his casual touches to arrange a fold of cloth or the position of an arm became more playful, caressing, lingering, and Jenny knew and didn't know what he was doing and why.

"Mind you, he never screwed her in the conventional

way," Jim said, refilling his glass to the brim. "Just went down on her and had her massage his back and legs, and, while she was in the vicinity, his prick and balls, the fucking bastard. They'd lie naked in that grove of his, where the sun broke through the leaves and the birds sang in the trees, and she did everything he wanted her to do and let him do anything he wanted to do. And you know what she says? She says she loved him. She'd loved her father when she was younger but now she loved only Bliss—I can't stand that goddamn name—only Bliss. And you know what goddamn Bliss does? He cans her dad. Not up to snuff, her dad, according to goddamn Bliss Fuckface's high standards. So it's 'Nice having known you and don't come to me for a letter of recommendation because I couldn't in good conscience write one.' Eckerman worked himself to death for him, but, you see, he just didn't produce the results, even screwed up once, supplied the professor with the wrong figures for a talk— embarrassed him to no end. So it's goodbye, David, and, incidentally, goodbye, Jenny, sweet Jenny, I'll miss you so, since David takes wife and kid and moves to L.A. And then the three of them live with her folks, who have tons of money but have to make sure he knows he's being a parasite, until he's had it and packs wife and kid off to a ghetto. For two years he tries to get admitted to grad school somewhere, moves from job to job, repairs Xerox machines, drives a delivery van, sends out thirty applications a month for a job in industry, keeps getting turned down by people who smell a rat. Meanwhile he drinks, is nasty to his wife and kid, rages at the bastard who ruined his career. Then, one fine day during an argument, Jenny tells him about her and the professor—costume parties, shady grove, sex and all. So what does

Eckerman do? Does he take the nearest plane, train, or tricycle and find the bastard and break every bone in his body? Nope. He runs out of the house, takes a beeline to the nearest railroad track and walks straight into the path of the next train to anywhere. That'll teach everybody, including his daughter. A few days later, she overhears a hushed conversation: they took her dad to the morgue in five pieces."

I heard myself groan.

Jim gave me a look of deep malice. "Now the mother, who hasn't given a shit about Jenny roughly forever, decides to go off the deep end and has to be locked up in the booby hatch. And Jenny is taken in by her loving grandparents. Suddenly she's in the lap of luxury. Best schools, riding lessons, designer wardrobe, servants. Does she care? She does not. She has other priorities. Gives Grandmother and Grandfather fits being Ms. Tomboy. And she wants to change her name. Never having cottoned to Daddy, they find that part agreeable. She's developed a taste for black humor, so she picks an uncle's last name because it's close enough to Latin for *death*, and she picks Vida, Spanish for *life*, for an ironic counter. Ten years later she finds that Vida is short for Davida—the feminine of David. So she didn't manage to dump dear old dad after all. Not that you're likely ever to dump somebody you think you've killed, right?" Jim emptied his glass and looked at me belligerently. "Right?"

I said nothing.

"Somebody else you're not likely to dump is somebody who tells you he loves you and teaches you about sex, and then stabs your father in the back and kicks you out. You hold on and you never ever let go. You marry a fucking professor, you write your thesis about a fucking scientist, you run after a fucking scientist to write a book about him and put him on a fucking pedestal. That's why there would never have been any point in my wooing her. I'm good enough to be let in on the deep dark secrets because I have empathy—that's what she says I have, and do I ever! She can tell me things when her husband is at the library busting his balls writing some hopeless book because he's just as hopeless a case as dear departed Dad. But that's all I'm good for, listening to her regurgitate the goddamn past. Remember what those fucking cards said about her? About the past being dead but strangling the present? They were right about that. It'll never let go of her because she'll never let go of it. And I'm just an idiot if I think she'll ever let go. I used to think that maybe if she could just get all that old garbage out by telling me about it she could put it behind her. Then I stopped believing that and settled for just being her empathetic buddy. Also her pathetic buddy, even if she didn't have a clue. You see, it gets more interesting: I knew her before New York." He paused and waited for me to react.

I said, "When?"

"Then. I knew her when she was twelve. That day when I saved your life, as you like to put it?—I recognized her on the street. You two were arguing and didn't notice me following you. I knew it was Jenny, I would have recognized her anywhere. Then numbnuts showed up with his paper cutter. Afterwards she didn't recognize me and I didn't want to say anything. It was a delicate matter, you see. I once spied on her and saw her in the grove with her professor. I was fourteen. This was the summer my parents were getting divorced and I was staying with my mother at an aunt's place. One day I was out front working on my aunt's car when Jenny bicycled by. We both said hello. A week later I saw her again, and this time she stopped and we talked for a while. She told me she'd just come from a photo session; she was a photographer's model and sat for him once a week. He lived half a mile down the road and was also a professor and her best friend. She laughed when she said 'photographer's model' like it was a joke she was letting me in on. After that I always tried to be outside when she bicycled by, and she always stopped and talked to me. And one day I ran after her because I wanted to see her photographer friend. I sneaked around the house and climbed a tree to peek over the wall in back. And there she was with him. They were both naked and he had his head between her legs.

"After that I couldn't get her out of my head. I thought about her all the time. She had this smile on her face, half pain and half bliss, when he was between her legs. I always remembered that smile. It hurt me, but in my mind I always went back to it. I still talked to her when she bicycled by, I waited all week for the day. I was fourteen, but I knew I loved her in a way I'd never love anybody else. Isn't that amazing? Isn't it?"

I was in no mood to agree. "Why in God's name didn't you tell her parents?"

Jim looked hurt. "I didn't know where they lived or who they were. She never talked about them. We talked about school and things we liked to do. The only adult she ever talked about was her professor, how they played chess and talked about all sorts of things, books, the stars, life and death—anything and everything. He was much more impor-tant to her than her parents. It bothered the hell out of me how important he was, but it never occurred to me to tell anybody about her and him. I never spied on her again. Then my mother found work in New York and we left. And brother, did it hurt to leave!"

Jim suddenly began to cry. "Ignore me, it's the booze," he said, and he sat, with both hands wrapped around his glass, while tears ran down his cheeks and dripped from his beard. "I never forgot her. I don't know why but I never did for a single day. When I saw her again I knew on that first day when we were having dinner that I still loved her. We started doing things together, and I was so happy because I was with her. I didn't mind that she was married to you. The only thing I minded was it showing me that anyone she'd be interested in had to be at least fifteen years older and a professor. Even if I turned myself into a professor, I couldn't fast forward myself and become older."

The pain under my sternum had spread thoughout my chest and had become linked with a dull, unfocused anger. "Did you tell her that you knew her then, as a kid? Does she know?"

Jim, wrapped up in self-pity, didn't seem to hear me. But then he reached for his pack, pulled a bandana from it and blew his nose. "No," he said.

"Why not?"

"I don't know. I didn't think it would matter to her. Why should she care?"

"Are you kidding? Why should she care that the one person in the world she's confiding in about what happened back then knew her back then?"

He shrugged and turned morose. "She doesn't give a shit about me."

"Aside from not being true, that's one hell of an excuse.

120

'She's not in love with me, so why should I tell her about something having to do with the most traumatic events of her life? Why not keep her in the dark so everything stays the same?'" Jim's refusal to tell Vida about his role in her past struck me as more monstrous than anything else he had told me, and as if I were slowly turning a knob, my anger began to focus on him. "What a terrific setup. She cries on your shoulder, you're her good buddy who pats her on the back and is all empathy, and nothing changes. Not a chance she'll figure out you've been in love with her all along. Not a chance she'll look at you and say, 'Christ, when all this happened he was a kid and so was I, and now he's going on thirty. And so am I.' No chance she'll figure out she's no longer the lonely waif who was hurt and betrayed and will accept the past as past and herself as an adult responsible for her own life. Let her forever be the child hugging its bruises and nursing its old grudges. She stays who she is and you remain in control of her emotional life."

Jim looked at me with exaggerated incredulity. "I don't believe this. Is this what Freud meant by paranoid projection? You're drawing a fucking self-portrait and you don't even know it. Control her? Not want her to change? How about not wanting her to have a single idea of her own? How about wanting her to stay exactly the way she was when you first laid eyes on her, not change a lock of hair on her fair head? The eternal adolescent, the wild young thing, the studious youth sitting at the feet of the mentor? You're the one who's doing everything in his power to keep her from growing up. You're the one who can't stand the thought of her writing her bloody book, going to bloody Italy—anything that suggests she may, just may, have a mind of her own or may, just

121

may, be changing. God knows what screwed you up so badly that you need her to stay exactly the way she is. Do you think I don't know why it's all right with you that I'm always around her? I spend as much time with her as you, and you, the guy she's married to, doesn't mind in the least. Doesn't that strike you as just a bit odd? Haven't you ever wondered why you don't mind? Because when she's with me she's the jock, the kid. She's the textbook case of arrested develop-ment, and no chance of any alarming change. So don't you accuse me of trying to control her. You're the biggest control freak I've met in my life."

For a fraction of a second muscles in my arm and shoulder contracted and my mind leaped ahead and rehearsed a punch at Jim's head, thrown as hard as I could. Then the impulse was gone and with it all my energy. I felt like lowering my head on my forearms and dropping into a black pit of exhaus-tion. I said, "So Freud died and made you head shrink."

He shook his head and all anger went out of him. "This psychological crap is useless when it comes to not getting terminally depressed," he said. "You can try to figure out what makes people tick until the cows come home and what counts is that she's found Fry, and on the daddy and A-num-ber-one authority figure front he fits the bill even better than you. Turns out I was wrong: he's the biggest control freak of them all; you can't hold a candle to him. He wants to control the frigging universe with that coincidence crap of his. And he has her jumping through hoops. He has her so wrapped around his little finger she's not giving anyone the time of day, not me nor, in case you hadn't noticed, you. It's all Geoff, Geoff, Geoff."

"For another week and a half."

"Are you sure about that? Are you absolutely sure she'll pack her bags and leave eminent and wise and scintillating Geoff?"

I said, "Nothing is absolute," and went to the bathroom. When I came back, Jim had turned on the TV and was singing along to the idiotic theme song of a game show.

Vida, returning around midnight, found us both drunk, watching a Kung Fu movie in Chinese with Italian subtitles. In the movie, two martial arts experts, one probably the good guy, the other probably the baddy, were competing for the favor of a woman who was either a hooker or the mistress and right hand of the ancient leader of a secret cult of knife-wielding cutthroats. Vida went to bed and Jim and I watched the movie to its surprise ending of all of the characters dying in a warehouse fire the woman had set.

6

IN THE MORNING I WOKE UP TO THE SOUNDS OF GURGLING gutters and steady rain, and to the hangover of hangovers. I crawled out of bed and padded to the living room. The place was deserted. In a note on the table, Jim informed me that he'd stop at the supermarket in the evening to buy groceries. Vida had obviously left for another day in the company of Fry. I swallowed a few aspirins and sat sipping black coffee, waiting for the pounding in my head to stop. I stared bleakly at the dark brew, my mind skimming over the night's revelations. No clear idea came out of the process, but I decided to say nothing to Vida about what Jim had told me until we were back in the States. More than ever I had the sense of our trip having been a mistake and there being something unhinged or warped about our stay in this place.

I tried to settle down to work but an hour later had gotten no further than a bleary-eyed rereading of a chapter of my manuscript. The din of the rain and rushing water distracted me, and I was about to crawl back into bed for some more sleep when I heard a car driving up outside and car doors opening and closing. A moment later Vida came in, followed by Fry. She was wearing his trench coat and carrying under her arm her mountain parka. My instant, heart-stopping fear was that they had come to tell me she was leaving me and would stay with him.

She said, "A funny thing happened to me on my way to the forum," and draped her parka over a chair. It was soaked, as were her pants and boots and her briefcase.

"There's been an accident," Fry explained. "The Fiat lost traction in a curve and got mired in a field. May I use your phone?"

While he looked through the phone book for the number of a garage and made a call, Vida, shivering but cavalierly flippant, told me that she'd been driving out to the duke's tower to help Geoff dismantle his experiment when she'd hit a puddle in a curve. The car had gone off the road and down an embankment—no more than a two-foot drop—just missing a large oak that could have ruined her whole day. She tried to get the car back on the road but got mired in the attempt. Then she walked the rest of the way to the tower, getting soaking wet. I noticed that she was pale, and I wondered how bad a scare she'd had.

Fry got off the phone and said somebody from the garage would be at the car in half an hour. Their tow truck was being worked on and all they'd be able to do was get the car back on the road. "Could you come with me and drive it back, John?" he asked.

"I can do it," Vida protested. "This wasn't the most traumatic experience of a lifetime."

"No, but you're wet and you got chilled. I want you to take a hot bath and get thoroughly warm again. I'll pick you up around two and we'll drive to the tower in my car. If you feel up to it."

I chafed at his easy familiarity, but she admitted that she was freezing and agreed to stay. She thanked Fry for the loan of his coat and handed it back to him. He put it on. "I couldn't have you come down with double pneumonia," he told her.

As soon as we'd gotten into the Mercedes, Fry said, "I don't want her near that car. She drives way too fast."

Again my hackles went up at his attitude of taking charge of Vida's well-being. "Lots of luck," I said. "It's not the easiest thing in the world to persuade her to do what's good for her. Not once she's made up her mind to do something truly dumb."

"She was badly shaken. She could easily have been killed," Fry said and looked at me from the side.

I tried to hide a feeling of sudden, intense weakness. "How do you know?" I asked.

"We stopped at the place on our way back to town and I took a look at the Fiat. The sideview mirror was torn off and there is a scrape along the entire length of the car. It's a massive tree. She was very, very lucky."

Vida was indeed very, very lucky. A blue smear of paint and a gouge marked where the car had squeezed past the oak. I picked up the mirror lying shattered in its twisted frame a few feet from the tree and put it in my pocket. Fry watched me and I expected him to say something about seven years of bad luck, but he only shivered deliberately and walked down the slope to the Fiat. He placed his hands on the roof and

127

looked inside through the window. "Minihearses, that's what many of these things turn into around here. Not to be morbid."

The rain had stopped but my shoes were soaked through and Fry suggested we sit in the Mercedes. "No point for the entire family to come down with galloping pneumonia."

The Fiat was not conspicuous from the road, but one of the few passing cars pulled over and stopped in front of the Mercedes. The young driver was a researcher at the Institute and knew Fry. Fry told him what had happened, and he said that some three or four years earlier a man and his wife had been killed on this very curve. After Fry's colleague had left, Fry said there probably wasn't a curve in all of the roads of Italy where there hadn't been at least one fatal accident.

The man from the garage appeared with a small truck, and using boards to get purchase under the tires of the Fiat, had little trouble pulling it out of the mire by its rear bumper. I thanked Fry for his help, said goodbye to him and drove to the villa, watching my speed on the wet road.

When I arrived, Vida had just gotten out of her bath. She wrapped her hair in a towel and went outside to look at the car. "I'll have to get the side repainted and get that fixed," she said, running a finger across the jagged stub where the side-view mirror had been. I took the battered remnant out of my pocket and showed it to her. She winced. "An inch closer and the car would have been a royal mess," she said.

I wondered whether she was thinking that two or three inches closer, not only the car would have been a mess. I said, "Don't catch your death out here with wet hair."

"True. One brush with death per day is enough." She went inside and dried her hair.

When she came into the living room after what seemed a long time, I asked her, "How are you feeling?"

She said, "Fine," and hurriedly went to her briefcase and opened it. "It's wet," she said. "Good thing it's waterproof." She stayed bent over it, her hand on the dark nylon as if she were studying it. A slight movement of her shoulders told me she was crying.

"What is it?" I asked.

She shook her head mutely and kept her face averted from me. I walked over to her and put my arm around her. But she shook her head again and began to rummage in her briefcase and pull folders from it. "I'm an idiot. I'm such an idiot," she said with so much anger in her voice that I thought I'd been mistaken and she hadn't been crying at all. But she was crying when she put the folders on the table. "And I never learn. That's the interesting thing. I don't ever learn."

"Is it Geoff?" I asked.

She finally looked at me and her anger shifted abruptly to me. "And you never learn either. That's the one thing we have in common. You're just as stupid."

"What is it I never learn?"

"There's no point," she said, sat down and began to leaf through her notes with a look of fierce concentration.

I went into the bedroom, sat on the bed and read pages in a book without the slightest idea of what I was reading.

Sometime later Vida came in. She said, "I'm sorry. I must have had a retroactive case of nerves." She sounded formal and remote.

"Are you all right now?" I asked.

"Yes, fine. I feel stupid, that's all. You'd think I'd have the brains to slow down without a Slippery When Wet sign." She avoided my eyes.

I brewed us some coffee, and we sat and talked about the country around Frascati, how often roads took unexpected turns for no apparent reason, and other innocuous topics. I felt we were both conscious of the fact that we were conducting a conversation that was as distant as Mars from what was on our minds and were powerless to change the script. But then Vida told an anecdote about one of the people at the Institute and laughed out loud in telling it, and when Fry stopped by a little later to pick her up, she seemed in fine spirits and joked about being on probation regarding the operation of motor vehicles. They left and I was once again baffled by a sense of having missed a cue or having responded to it in an inappropriate way.

In the evening Jim was served a matter-of-fact, nothing-to-it, happens-all-the-time version of the accident. He couldn't resist pointing out that the reason it happened all the time here was that everybody here thought they were in the Indy 500.

Vida didn't make the obvious retort about accidents not being entirely unknown in the U.S. of A. "At least it makes life interesting. You have to admit that," she said.

"Sure," he agreed. "Nothing like living on the edge of terror—knowing that any instant you may be a charred corpse. Talk about a cheap thrill."

But Vida ignored the jab and began talking about Fry, who, she said, was driving her crazy: He was in the middle of one of his experiments and refused to let her in on it because talking about it might bias its outcome. In addition to his office, he had a lab in a remote corner of the Institute and there was a room full of instruments—oscilloscopes, panels of lights, computers—he tinkered with. He told her that she was welcome to watch, but otherwise the only thing she knew was that at the heart of the experiment was a gadget registering radioactive decay.

I said that Fry was certainly versatile—from the tarot to radioactive decay in the blink of an eye.

"He's brilliant," Vida said. "He can work on three things at once and never lose track of any of them. He remembers everything you tell him, even the minutest detail. He's amazing."

The next day, again left to myself at the villa, while Vida was with brilliant, amazing Geoffrey Fry, and Jim was in Rome with his heartache, I became oppressed by the quiet. Jim's revelations and accusations wormed their way into my mind and made concentration on the pages before me impossible. I tried to dismiss his charges as unfair and evidence that he didn't know me at all; he was using half-baked textbook psychology to pigeonhole me—an enterprise guaranteed to simplify anyone beyond recognition. Nor did he know Vida, who had not, of that I was very sure, fallen in love with me and married me out of some never-to-be satisfied need for a father. But try as I might to shrug off Jim's accusations, they kept having the feel of a wound of whose extent and potential to hurt me, once some self-protective anesthetic had worn off, I was afraid.

I decided to fight my mood by taking a walk. The day was cold and there was a drizzle off and on. After a tour of the

EVELIN SULLIVAN

roads around the main piazzas, I found the park where Fry
and I had observed the children in their carnival costumes a
week and a half earlier. I walked down its length and discovered a remarkable sight: a large fountain set into a hillside,
dry but with basin above basin marching like giant gray steps
up the hill, each designed to catch water from the one above
it, in one cascading waterfall after another. At the bottom
was a long wall of alcoves in which heads of tritons were
ready to spout water from their mouths into a moat running
along the base of the wall. In the moat were rusty pipes and
valves, and debris and litter. Batteries of floodlights mounted on two poles and trained on the fountain made me try to
imagine it on a summer night, with gushing and gurgling
water glittering in the blaze, but all I saw was desolation and
ruin, moss-covered basins, stone faces disfigured by age and
dark water stains, rust eating at the stubs of pipes protruding
from their mouths. Stairs were skirting the basins on either
side, but access to them, through two short tunnels in the
bottom wall, was closed off with iron gates and I had to
climb the hill along a wire-mesh fence. On top, the main
basin was empty and covered with lichen, and the fence kept
sightseers away from a balustrade overlooking the fountain
and park. I was alone but for a jogger who presently came
trotting up one of the paths and passed me without giving me
a glance. On the way down the hill, I was attacked by a sadness so all-pervasive that I resolved to call Vida the moment
I was back at the villa, not in order to tell her how I felt but
to hear her voice and know that she was near.

But when I got back I thought that Vida wouldn't know
what to make of a call out of the blue, and I tried to do some
writing. I hadn't gotten very far when I had a speak-of-the-

132

devil surprise visitor: Geoffrey Fry. He buzzed me and I had to go outside and open the gate for him. I asked him at once where Vida was.

He said, "Are we beginning to look like Siamese twins? I've left my other self—I should say my infinitely more attractive self—at the library with a list of things to look up for me. A low ruse, I'm afraid, but I'd like you to participate in an experiment, and the result might be compromised if she knew. I apologize for this being such short notice."

I wondered whether he expected me to comment on his reference to Vida's attractiveness. If he did, I disappointed him. I told him that I'd been getting on my own nerves anyway and welcomed a distraction. He said the experiment was at the Institute. For a change? I asked. He laughed and said, "Those were experiments with quotation marks around them; this one is a bona fide, on the cutting edge of science, experiment."

Before we reached the Institute, he thought of something. He pulled over to the side of the road and asked me to move to the backseat and lie down and cover myself with a blanket. Otherwise he'd have to get a pass for me, which always took forever. I followed his instructions, and Fry breezed through the gate, shouting a cheerful "*buon giorno*" at the guards. He drove a short distance and stopped the car in a grove shielding his lab, a small, low building. Next to it was a substation that hummed and crackled inside a high cyclone fence.

"There should be nobody around," Fry said when we got out of the car. "My lone assistant is spending the week at a conference in Padua." He unlocked the door and we entered a long corridor, doors on either side. "Offices on the left, labs on the right," he briefed me. He opened one of the doors on the right, and met by the hum of fans we entered a dimly lit, windowless room cluttered with several computers, electronics equipment, nests of cables and other gadgetry, most of which made no sense to me. At the center of the room stood two old-fashioned wooden chairs with high backs and armrests. Facing them was a large wheel, its rim studded with small light bulbs.

"Don't tell me—radioactive decay," I said.

"Do I have an informant in my ranks, and what else has she told you?" he asked.

"Only that security is tight."

"Never trust anyone with a note pad." Fry pressed a button on a panel and the top light on the wheel came on bright and yellow. "It's true that if any of this should fall into the wrong hands, irreparable damage would be done to national security," he said, indicating the equipment with a sweeping gesture. "Especially the power supplies and cable ties." He typed an instruction on the keyboard of one of the computers and columns of numbers began to race up the amber screen of the monitor. He stopped their progress, checked the bottom reading, started the process again. "But seriously, folks. A similar setup was used decades ago to study psychokinesis. Except, the people who did the study knew appallingly little about the statistics of randomness."

On the wheel, the light at the top went off and one next to it came on. A few seconds later that one went off and its neighbor came on. Then it went off and the top light came on again. The same thing was repeated in the opposite direction. After watching for a minute, the impression I had was that of a single light marching two or three steps clockwise or counterclockwise and then jumping back to the twelve o'clock position.

Fry was still studying his numbers, but he continued his explanation. "The question was whether the attempt to mentally influence a random process would make it nonrandom. Let's say you flipped a coin a hundred times and recorded whether it landed heads or tails. If the coin is balanced, you should on average get fifty heads and fifty tails. Of course the likelihood is high that you'll get either two heads or two tails in a row for any two tosses, but in the long run the numbers of heads and tails will even out. If you think of it in terms of how many of the same side will come up consecutively, two of the same in a row is very likely, three in a row less, and as that number grows, the likelihood of consecutive agreement decreases dramatically. Even if you did a thousand tosses, the odds against getting twenty heads or tails in a row is a million to one. Now suppose that every time you tossed the coin you wished for heads to come up. The question is, would that increase the number of times in a row you'd get heads?"

"You mean would I use some mental power I don't know anything about to reach in and somehow pull on the coin while it's spinning in the air to make it fall heads up? Even though I can't even see which side is heads?"

"That's one way of looking at it. Not, as you've just pointed out, a particularly satisfying one."

"But according to your coincidence theory, some acausal force would produce a correlation between what's in my mind and how the coin lands."

For some reason Fry seemed taken aback. "You've done extracurricular work," he said. He seemed on the verge of adding something but checked himself. "You're essentially right. But the coin toss is just an example. It's too crude to detect what is probably a very subtle effect. That's where

135

radioactive decay comes in. When an atom decays isotropically, it emits radiation randomly in any direction. If you mount two identical detectors opposite each other and position a radiation source exactly between them, each detector should pick up the identical number of radiated particles if the sampling is over a sufficiently long time, and although one detector may get two or three or more hits in a row, the likelihood of a given number of consecutive hits on it drastically decreases with the number. For a thousand emitted particles the chance of twenty in a row striking one of the detectors is one in a million."

"Unless something biases the process."

"Exactly."

Fry explained the wheel with its traveling and jumping light: The radioactive source emitted a particle every three or so seconds on average. For each hit on, say, the right detector, the light would travel one step in the clockwise direction. But the moment the sequence was interrupted by a hit on the left detector, the light would jump back to the top of the wheel. And the same held for the left side of the wheel. Since there were twenty bulbs for each semicircle, the twentieth being the shared bottom bulb, the odds for the light reaching the bottom of the wheel by chance was one in a million.

"The game is the following. Pick a side and try to force the light to travel around your half of the wheel by wishing it to go around your half. You can use any mental trick—imagine you're seeing the light go in your direction or imagine you're turning on the light you want to come on, or whatever. Which side do you choose?"

I chose the right side probably because I felt more comfortable thinking clockwise than counterclockwise. Fry indicated the right chair and I sat down after following Fry's example and taking off coat and sweater. He wired up my wrists and head with electrodes connected to velcro-covered straps. "No observation without a zillion monitors," he said. "In this business you don't believe you've blown your nose unless you see a readout." He sat down in the left chair and wired himself up. "I'll be doing the same thing with the left side, so it'll really be a tug-of-war. We'll keep at it until one of us gives out, which should be in less than an hour since I expect us to concentrate fiercely. But anyone who gets all the way to the bottom is the instant winner and all-time champion."

I had been watching the light throughout Fry's explanation and had not seen it go beyond five in a row on either side before jumping back to the top. Fry flicked a few switches, checked a dial and waited for the light to jump back to the top. "Now," he said. "Good luck, John."

The light jumped to his side one step, two steps, and I imagined leaping in, grabbing it with my right and pulling it in my direction. It leaped out of my hand even further left and I grabbed it again and tugged with all my might. It suddenly gave and jumped back to the top. I kept pulling toward my side, dislodged it and moved it one step. But then it shot through my hand and was at the top of the wheel again.

Fry had been right, the game was a tug-of-war: as it progressed, sweat began to run down my chest, and I felt the strain in my hand and arm. I'd pull, move the light a notch or two or even three. Then it would either suddenly yield and jump to the top if it had been on his side, or be yanked out of my hand and leap to the top if it had been on mine. My hand and arm became sore from being tense. I lost track of time, forgot why I was working like a fiend at something I had no control over according to the known laws of the universe. What mattered was to get the light to come my way, and I pulled and pulled until I was trembling with the strain.

Throughout this, I was hardly aware of Fry next to me. What took over my mind instead was the sense of a malevolent force bent on frustrating my aim, single-mindedly committed to making me fail. As I kept struggling, I began hating my enemy and fearing him. I strained and pulled, furious at never getting the light to move more than four steps in my direction before it flicked through my hand, terrified when it worked its way along the other side of the rim and no amount of effort kept it from taking three, four, five steps. When it would finally yield and jump back to the top of the wheel there was an instant of relief, as if I had narrowly escaped disaster, but the struggle continued.

There came a moment when I felt I had been doing this forever. There had never, not as long as I could remember, been a time when I had not fought a force that was bent against me with the blind will to foil my aims, thwart me, sneer at my deepest desires. Except I was finally about to lose, and the fight would be over for all time. I felt dizzy and faint. The light and my effort to control it were being swallowed up by a gray haze. I was glad that I'd be able give up fighting and lie down in that haze, safe in the peace of utter ruin. But suddenly an image appeared before my inner eye: an image of the wheel, the light at its bottom shining a bright yellow. My dizziness left me and was replaced by a calm awareness of my surroundings. With this awareness came a sense of perfect ease and the confidence of certainty. The mental image was gone, and I watched—as if I were observing an event I had already seen—the light travel in my direction along the side of the wheel. Five steps out along the wheel, another five on its way down, another five still down and curving inward. There were four steps left, then three, then two.

But suddenly Fry was on his feet, throwing a switch on a panel and tearing off the bands around his wrists and head. He grabbed a wrench on a table, quickly stepped over to the wheel and violently struck the bottom light just as it came on. The blow knocked the bulb and socket out of the wheel, but dangling from a wire, the bulb kept shining. Fry backed away from it and stood staring at it. Then he turned to the computer screen. He looked ghastly. He had sweated patches on his shirt and sweat had run down his face to his collar.

"I had no idea the supernatural could be so exhausting," I said.

He looked at me with a dazed expression as if he had heard nonsense sounds from my direction and went back to looking at the screen. Studying columns of numbers, he began to swear in a low voice in Italian. I wondered whether I could take off the experimental paraphernalia but decided to wait for him to tell me. He stopped swearing but kept staring at the numbers. I had the feeling he was no longer seeing them but was trying to regain his composure. Finally, he said to the screen, "That's astounding. Absolutely astounding." Then he turned to me. "What happened to you when the light started going your way?" Noticing that I was still wired up, he added, "Here, let me help you with that."

"I don't know. I felt faint. I imagined the light at the bottom lit. And then I had a feeling the light would come in my direction. I seemed to know it would."

Fry shook his head. "*Astounding* is the word. Take it from me. The universe is a grade-A bastard." He removed the straps from around my wrists and head.

I said, "Wasn't this what you were looking for? Coincidence, correlation by affinity? The mind biasing the outcome of random events? You don't seem pleased."

"Are you trying for understatement of the year or just being polite? To answer your question, Yes, this was what I was looking for, with one notable difference: I wanted to win. The shocking truth is I've never been a gracious loser. I rigged it up this way because I thought there might be more energy in the system if it were a battle of minds rather than one mind trying to control the light. So, of course, I get emotionally involved and turn it into a matter of life and death. And what happens? The cosmos thumbs its nose at me. Try all you want, fool—you still lose, it says."

He made a few entries in a logbook, turned off the light on the wheel, dangling from its wire, and with me once again hiding under the blanket, we left the Institute and Fry took me to a pizzeria and treated me to lunch. Although the experiment already seemed quaint, and the degree to which I had gotten caught up in it quainter, winning the battle of the wheel had for the moment gotten rid of my depression. I joked about the colossal effort the clash of the Titan minds had been and asked Fry whether he'd be able to use its result as proof of his theory, my name being of course prominently featured in the learned paper he'd submit to the Academy of Science. He said not unless others, repeating the experiment, obtained the same results, and we fell into a discussion about how purported scientific discoveries acquired legiti-macy. But I felt he was distracted throughout the meal and became interested in the conversation only when, apropos possible fraudulent or biased experiments, I asked him what-ever happened to his predecessor, the Austrian biologist.

"Kammerer?" he said. "He killed himself. Shot himself through the temple at forty-five—in the Alps, I believe. Couldn't live with the ruin of his scientific reputation, the fool."

"Why 'the fool'?"

"Because losing your reputation isn't worth dying for—make a note of that—and because he had no idea of what to do with what he'd found."

"And you do?"

"I'm beginning to doubt it."

He sounded tired and dispirited, and I felt a twinge of pity for him. "Maybe it's one of those things it's not a good idea to do anything with," I offered. "Maybe you're better off just marveling at it."

"Words of wisdom," he said. "But I don't think I have a choice in the matter. If you're starving and you're offered food that may be poisoned, you eat it, don't you?"

"You could wait in the hope that something better will come along."

"Suppose you're unable to hope?"

"I don't know. It might help if I knew what we're talking about."

He laughed. "Interestingly enough, it wouldn't." He paused, apparently pondering what he had said, then he abruptly asked me, "Do you love Vida?"

I had gotten used to his quick changes of tack, but this one caught me off guard. For an instant I had the impression that we were back in the lab, battling for domination of the roving light. "Yes," I said. "Do you?"

He pulled back and said, "Ha—tit for tat," and after a pause, "What would you say if I told you yes?"

"I'd say you're wrong. You may be in love with her, but you don't love her."

"A lesson in semantics?"

"A crucial difference."

He laughed again. "You know, it has occurred to me that in another life we might have been friends."

"I doubt it. I like my friends honest."

I didn't know what had made me say something so insulting and I was about to apologize, but Fry didn't seem offended. "A greatly overrated concept, honesty," he said.

"Then there's no point in asking you whether you're in love with Vida."

"Because you couldn't trust my answer to be honest?"

"Why should I, under the circumstances."

"The 'circumstances' meaning my possible lack of commitment to honesty or my possible unwillingness to reveal the status of my emotional life regarding Vida?"

"Either."

"OK, honestly. I think she is lovely and lovable. There have been times in these past weeks when she's made me very happy. Does that mean I'm in love with her?"

I was tempted to ask him what particular times he was referring to and whether they had been in any way connected with a bed at his house or a couch in his office. But all I said was, "Maybe."

"Then I'm maybe in love with her. These things do happen

to us whether they're convenient—or socially acceptable—or not. Do you think she's in love with me? Honestly now, since we're suddenly up to our ears in the moral life."

"Maybe. But if she is, that won't change anything. She'll go back to New York with me."

"Because she loves you? Or is in love with you?"

"Because she believes in loyalty. She won't leave me for a momentary infatuation."

"Another greatly overrated concept. It's amazing how many of them there are. I should compile a list."

He spoke slowly, and I felt he was paying only minimal attention to what he was saying while his mind was on other things. "Loyalty or infatuation?" I asked. He didn't answer. "Name a concept that isn't greatly overrated according to your view of the cosmos," I challenged him. "And coincidence doesn't count because it's too obvious."

He came back from wherever he had been. "As in 'Death where is thy sting'? Also too obvious." He checked his watch. "How about time? As a concept. Speaking of which, I had better return to my dubious devices and let you get on with Great-uncle Anders. No rest for the weary."

"Not until they're six feet underground under a five-hundred-pound slab."

Fry was taking money from his wallet. He stopped and sat motionless, his eyes on the bills in his hand, as if suddenly paralyzed. I thought of his terror of death and regretted what I had said. "I'm sorry, I didn't mean to be ghoulish," I apologized.

He slowly raised his eyes, and for a moment I thought I saw tears in them. But he said with mock solemnity and a gentleness that startled me, "You're too kind for this world,

143

my friend. What will protect you from its wickedness?"

For some reason, his calling me his friend pleased me, and it occurred to me that contrary to the known rules of human relationships, according to which I should resent and loathe a rival in love, I liked him. "Clean living?" I suggested.

He laughed. "No doubt."

He drove me back to the villa. When I got out of the car, he said, "In all the excitement I forgot to congratulate you on winning. I'm glad you did. Honestly. Congratulations."

When Jim came home in the evening after his day in Rome, I told him about the wheel of lights. He was in his usual bad mood, but listened to my story with a minimum number of snide remarks, although he did conclude that Fry was mad as a March hare.

I pointed out that genius has not infrequently been mistaken for lunacy.

"Yes, but where is it written that you can't be a genius and a lunatic at the same time?" he countered. "What was he monitoring anyway, pulse rate? beta waves? If he believes in his correlation force, all that biological shit shouldn't even enter the picture."

"I suppose he has to measure something if he wants to treat it as science. Anyway, he's very bright and he may just know what he's doing without necessarily letting us know."

"Now don't you start. I've had it up to here with Vida gushing. As if nobody else in the world ever had a brain, or used it for anything more ambitious than figuring out how to tie his shoelaces. And we're so incredibly privileged because we know him, and he talks to us, and plays the piano for us, and even lets us participate in his experiments."

Vida came home full of news about the assassination of a prominent government figure, and we turned on the TV and got into a discussion about Italian politics and the Mafia—subjects infinitely less volatile than Geoffrey Fry. I don't know why I didn't tell her then or in the morning about Fry's experiment and my role in it. Maybe I wanted to avoid or postpone her probable reaction of jealousy at his having chosen me instead of her. Or maybe I was simply tired of talk about Fry and not interested in the hour-long discussion that would ensue if I mentioned our battle waged for the greater glory of science.

I DON'T KNOW AT WHAT POINT IN OUR ITALIAN HOLIDAY I began to feel that I was in a race against time. I do know that after Vida's accident I became aware of a by then well-developed fear—as if I had randomly run my fingers across my abdomen and with a cold shock had suddenly felt a swelling that had to have been there for some time. The fear—one I had not told Fry about because lying was fair in love and war and because I wanted to believe in the loyalty of the woman I loved—was that each day Vida was moving further away from me and that, if nothing changed, she would, after x more days of exposure to Fry, be so distant that no effort on my part would return her to me. The morning after the wheel of lights, the question I asked myself was whether x was shorter or longer than our much-too-slowly dwindling number of days at Frascati. If it was shorter, the return ticket in her briefcase would, I was convinced, be a useless piece of paper; if it was longer, we'd be on our way home in a week and two days and I'd be able to write off Fry as Vida's second straying, consummated or not, from the matrimonial straight and narrow. I'd pick up my bruised self, check for breaks and open wounds, and consider myself lucky to have survived relatively unscathed.

I mentally compiled a list of things for and against me. In my favor was that Vida had put behind her her chemistry professor, a man who had fit to a T Jim's description of the type of man she was drawn to—an authority figure, a scientist, someone a quarter of a century older than she. Against me was that Fry probably had ten times the prestige, charm, wit and seductiveness of that earlier infatuation. Against me was also that Vida had seemed to be moving away from me by her own accord for the last year or so. Aside from her loyalty, which I did not finally believe in, the only other thing in my favor, although it flew in the face of the evidence, was an embattled conviction that Vida did care about me.

As far as Fry's role in all this went, his confession that he hated to lose acquired an ominous ring in my memory. Once I replayed what we had talked about after the experiment, no time at all was needed for me to see it as a hidden warning that he meant to win Vida from me—which, in light of the pattern Jim had revealed to me, seemed like a joke on him, since he could have no idea of how vulnerable she was to a man meeting certain criteria that had been branded into her child's brain by the man who had replaced and then killed her father.

✳

After two unexpected interruptions on two consecutive days, I should have anticipated a third one on the third day. The surprise visitor was Jim, out of breath and barely able to contain himself. "I have news—big news," he said. "Hold on to your hat. I did some thinking last night and some pretty amazing things occurred to me. So I checked them out this morning. You'll never believe where I went."

I was irritated by his I-got-a-secret attitude. "OK, I don't believe where you went."

"I went to see Signor Valga. Remember Signor Valga, the fortuneteller with all the good news? I asked him for a reading."

"Why?"

"To break the ice. I wanted to get information out of him. Plus I thought it wouldn't hurt to get some idea of what sulphur pits lie ahead for yours truly."

"I thought you didn't believe in the tarot."

"I don't know what I believe anymore. Ever since we arrived in this godforsaken country there hasn't been a day when I haven't felt weird. And now it turns out I had every right to feel weird."

"What did the reading say?"

"I don't mean the reading. That was standard stuff: I'll learn something startling in the near future. I'll have to make a vital choice. There'll be a change. Then I pumped Valga about Fry. I assumed he'd be reluctant to talk about a client, so I was the soul of diplomacy. I told him I was impressed by how much Fry knew about the tarot. Valga almost went through the roof. All Fry knows is surface, he said. He wants to use the tarot as a map to the future, but that's just one thing the tarot is. The true tarot leads to spiritual understanding, blah, blah, but it takes courage to go on that journey. I asked him why Fry was so interested in the future, and he said, 'Because he's afraid.' 'Of what?' I asked. He clammed up. He didn't know, he said; people are afraid of many things. So I got clever. I took the tarot cards and spread them out face up. Then I pointed at one and asked, 'Is he afraid of that?' The card was the Devil. He shook his head and collected the cards, didn't say a word. I was about to give up and leave, but he fanned the deck, picked a card and tossed it on the table. Can you guess which one?"

"Death on a pale horse."

Jim pulled back startled. "How did you know?"

"He and I talked about death the night of the readings. I couldn't sleep and went back to Valga's place. Fry was there having the cards read."

"Talk about insisting on knowing the future!"

"Afterwards he told me he was terrified of death."

"Which brings us to Discovery Two. Tell me, when you went to the Institute yesterday, did Fry get a pass for you at the gate?"

"No. I hid under a blanket. It takes forever to get a pass."

"So nobody knew you were there. That makes sense. That experiment yesterday? The wheel of lights—step right up, folks—clash of the mental giants? He tried to kill you. If you hadn't won, you would have died."

I heard Jim say it, and part of me believed him instantly. But another part was all common sense and disbelief. "You're not serious!"

"Sounds crazy, doesn't it? But that's what I keep telling you, Fry is crazy. Everything you told me last night about that experiment smelled wrong. It kept bothering me, and finally I figured out what the setup reminded me of—a couple of electric chairs. So I went to the Institute after I was through with Valga and climbed the fence and found Fry's building. He had you hooked up to enough amperage to fry you, no pun intended. Himself too, so I suppose he persuaded himself that he was being scrupulously fair, cosmic-influence-wise. Except he didn't have the nerve to see it through when things went against him. If he hadn't killed the circuit before that bottom light came on, he would have had ten amps go through him."

I remembered the feel of the straps around my wrists and saw in my mind a picture of a man's body arched in an electric chair, smoke rising from him. I said, "I don't understand. Why would he want to kill me or risk killing himself?"

"I don't know, but it's bound to have something to do with that correlation or coincidence craziness of his and with his terror of *La Morte*. Remember our first night here? The tower with the dead lovers and the dead duke? Why show us that and tell us the story? And why schlepp us to a tarot reading—all those fucking cards about death and disaster? And let's not forget that he made sure Vida had a small car and showed her how to drive it like a maniac."

"But he couldn't have foreseen the accident," I protested.

"Not foreseen, but how about wished?"

"That would be insane!"

"And trying to get you killed by some cosmic force that mucks about with radioactive decay isn't?"

From nowhere I had a mental image of the blue Fiat wrapped around the oak like crinkled aluminum foil. "I have to find Vida," I said.

"Ah, which brings us to Discovery Number Three. Before

I left, I overheard her and Fry what is in polite circles called making love in an office across the hall.——I'm sorry, I thought you should know."

I felt lightheaded and detached from myself. "You should have warned her," I said, wondering whether acute pain always felt like this at first.

"What, after knocking politely on the door?"

I doggedly tried to think. "He's dangerous," I said. "She shouldn't be with him."

"She may disagree. Long-distance sex can be so unsatisfying."

His baiting me helped me orient myself. "Goddammit, it doesn't matter what they're doing. If you're right about him, she's in danger. I don't give a damn whether they're screwing their brains out." The bald-faced lie had the effect of further steadying me. "I'll call Fry and tell him that we know everything. He won't dare do anything if he knows that we know."

Jim wasn't convinced. "I think we ought to get out of here in a hurry. There's no telling what he may dream up next. I'll pack and call the airline."

I found Fry's number on a sheet of paper and dialed it. Fry answered the phone after the first ring. I suddenly didn't know how to begin. "Geoff, it's John," I said.

"John, that's a surprise. What can I do for you?"

His glibness gave me nerve. "You can stop trying to kill me, for a start," I said.

There was a pause at the end of the line. Then Fry asked, "Where are you?"

"At the villa," I said. "With Jim."

He laughed. "Is that where the melodrama originated,

with the mighty Mr. Quarrel infiltrating enemy territory?" There was another pause. "All right, you do deserve some answers. I tell you what, why don't you meet me at the *gelateria* on the square. We can have an espresso and talk."

"About what? Why you didn't succeed in electrocuting me?"

"That and other salient questions."

His coolness unnerved me. "Is Vida there? Let me talk to her."

"No." The reply was flat and categorical. "Not until we've had our talk. I'll see you on the piazza in ten minutes." He hung up.

Jim had listened to my end of the conversation. "I'm coming with you," he said after I had filled in Fry's side.

"No," I said. "You pack our stuff and get us on a plane out of here. Whatever he's up to, he isn't going to pull a gun or a knife on me."

✳

By the time I got to the *gelateria* Fry was already there, seated at one of the outdoor tables. He had ordered two espressos, and they stood steaming on the glass table top. "I didn't know how many lumps," he said and pointed at the sugar bowl.

I looked at the black broth and had the crazy thought that it might be poisoned.

"It isn't poisoned—in case you're wondering," Fry said.

I sat down. "What I'm wondering is whether you tried to kill me. Did you try to kill me?"

He took a sip from his cup. "Careful, it's hot," he warned me, and settled back in his chair. "To answer your question:

Strictly speaking, yes. But, also strictly speaking, not directly. I deliberately put you in harm's way and hoped harm
would come your way. So there was malevolence in the original sense of *volere male*, wanting ill, and it's a dreadful thing
to have to admit to that. But let me tell you a story and
maybe all of this will make some sense. It's not a long story
but it's a sad one.

"Once upon a time there was a man who was afraid of
death—all the storytelling skill in the world won't give you
an idea of how greatly. He was afraid because he'd once been
dead briefly and had not liked it at all. The problem was that
after he almost died, he found signs wherever he looked
telling him that soon he'd be dead forever. There'd always be
a black cross, or a skull, or words like *cadaver* or *corpse* or *coffin* jumping into his path. One day he went to a tower that
had an evil reputation and asked a fortuneteller there, 'Does
all this mean I'll die soon?' The fortuneteller looked at his tea
leaves—"

"Tarot leaves," I interrupted him.

He bowed his head. "Looked at his tarot leaves and said,
'Maybe yes and maybe no. You or someone like you will surely die, but if the someone like you dies then it won't be you
who dies. Remember, everything a man has will he give for
his life.' The man went home and thought about this, but he
was distracted by a letter he got in the mail. Now this was a
very interesting letter because of the name of its writer and
a mistake in it. The name, translated into English, was Life
Death, and the mistake was that the writer, instead of writing
as she had intended, 'If I could arrange a way of seeing you,
would you be willing to cooperate with me?,' had written, 'If
I could arrange a way of *being* you . . .'

"The man thought, This is remarkable—someone who is life and death and who wants to arrange a way of being me. Surely this is worth a look."

I interrupted him. "So the story about how you found the sheet with the Morse code and so forth was a lie."

"An unavoidable distortion. All right, a lie. The effect was the same: the coincidences were what made me invite Vida."

"Which you did, hoping that the grim reaper would pick her instead of you. Coincidence—correlation by affinity."

"It was nothing in the least personal. How could it have been? She was just words on a sheet of paper. But then things became muddled. Instead of coming alone she brought you, who had a career tainted by accusations of unethical conduct like our biologist friend Kammerer. And she brought Jim Quarrel, whose last name is an arrow, *la sagitta*, which in the early tarot was what is now The Tower, and who had saved your life by coincidentally being at the right place at the right time. As far as I could tell, there suddenly were three candidates for the one role. Valga's readings were no help. According to them, any one of you could have qualified as my substitute."

"So you just sat back and waited for one of us to be chosen once the universe recognized some likeness to you or some correlation with your life. Except you didn't just sit back and wait: you must have been heartbroken when Vida didn't run the Fiat head-on into that tree."

Fry shook his head violently before I had finished. "No I wasn't. You have to believe that. I didn't want her to be the one. Not once I began to know her. I'm not a monster."

"You mean once you began having sex with her?"

He pulled back into himself. "This is the day for discoveries," he said and took another sip of espresso. "Well, you already knew I was in love with her. What else do you know?"

"What else is there to know?"

He studied me for a moment then said, "I suppose there is no harm in telling the truth. That she knew me as a child. Or did she tell you? I don't suppose she did."

An abyss yawned at my feet, and I pitched forward and fell through a whirl of images. I saw the figure of evil that Jim had conjured up—the naked satyr bent over a naked child. I saw it merge with the man before me. I saw Fry, naked, fondling a child; Vida, naked, being fondled by a lecher.

"She doesn't know I recognized her," Fry continued when I didn't answer. "But I did a few days after the tarot readings. It's astounding how you can not think about something for years and years and suddenly it flicks into your mind and takes away your breath. We were at the cafeteria. She was looking at a man playing with a puppy. She was smiling, and all at once that smile brought her back to me the way she was then. Do you know anything about her childhood?"

I couldn't speak.

"You do. Did she tell you? Did she present the two of us, her and me, as your typical childhood trauma requiring years of therapy before there is any hope of recovery? Did she? What she probably forgot to mention was that I loved her. You may choose to disbelieve this, but I was never a child molester—with one notable exception, obviously. There was never anyone but her. For two years I loved that child with an intensity and devotion I hadn't thought possible. I loved her more than I loved anyone before or after. But for close to two years I didn't touch her. We hugged, we kissed each other, I photographed her in the nude, but there was such an amazing feeling of something untarnished in everything we did. I regret what finally happened, but given the same circumstances again, I'm not sure it would be within my power to change anything. But even then there was an innocence at the heart of it."

"So much innocence that it ended up killing her father."

Fry seemed disappointed at my lack of empathy. He leaned back and shook his head. "Her father would have been a mediocre scientist at best. I was sorry when I heard of his death. But there was nothing I could have done. After I fired him, he could have found an assistantship with another adviser. If he'd had the drive, he could have gone on in the profession. Mediocrities thrive. Even in science there is always some backwater where they can paddle about. He could have had a career if he'd tried. Instead of sitting around until he was finally overcome by self-pity and convinced himself he had to take himself out of the picture."

My anger was as sudden as it was intense, but I spoke slowly for the sake of emphasis. "That's not why he killed himself," I said. "He walked in front of a train because she told him about you and her. That's what he couldn't stand. He admired you and thought he had a future in your field, and then you fired him. But he survived that. What he didn't survive was finding out that his admired adviser had diddled his little daughter and that he'd let it happen."

Fry's face had become a slack mask, but he quickly recovered. "Then he was an even greater fool. I didn't harm Jenny. If he killed himself because she told him about us, all that means is that he used what happened between her and me as an excuse to do away with himself. What happened between her and me was private. It doesn't matter how sordid it may strike other people—her pathetic father, you, anyone else—it wasn't. Not to us."

"Her pathetic father should have gone after you with a baseball bat. He should have caved in your skull. She was a little kid with parents who gave her nothing, and then she found you. You took advantage of her need and her vulnerability. You used her and you harmed her, and when you were through with her, you threw her out with her father. Didn't you ever think about what it did to her when you fired him? When she knew she wouldn't be able to see you any longer?"

Fry shook his head. "I had no choice. David kept making mistakes—costly mistakes. And I knew that the time had come to put an end to what was going on between her and me. What we had couldn't have survived much longer. She was changing. In the fall she was going to a new school. It was time for her to start leading a different life, a normal life. That's what we want for our children, isn't it? A normal life. Education, profession, marriage, what have you. And that's pretty much what happened, isn't it?"

I said, "Is that a rhetorical question, or are you seriously suggesting that her obsession with the past is normal?"

"Obsession is a strong word."

"Then what do you call her fascination with scientists, when she doesn't have a scientific bone in her body. And how do you explain the small matter of sex with scientists? You're not her first extramarital fling with a member of the tribe, in case she forgot to tell you. Not to mention the professor angle—me. And why did she want to see you again after all these years? Why this enormous interest in writing a book about you? Because she's never gotten over what you did to her."

Fry waited until I stopped talking. Then he took another sip of espresso and said, "Did I mention that I believe psychic trauma to be the century's single most overrated concept?" When I didn't answer, he said, "All right, I *have* asked myself to what extent the book was a ploy to see me. My guess, and you won't like to hear this because it's too unsoulwrenching, is that she still had feelings for me and was reminded of them when she read about me in that article. But she was afraid to write to me and let me know about her. So the book became a legitimate excuse that she herself could believe in."

"You must be out of your mind. She thinks she killed her father because of what happened between you and her. You can't seriously think for a second that she read about you in that journal and saw your picture, and suddenly her little heart went pitter-patter and she thought how nice it would be to see you again."

"The imbecilic expressions aside, why not?"

"Because that's not who she is. You're talking about someone who hasn't been able to let go for a second of what happened to her fifteen years ago. It's not a question of the occasional bittersweet reverie. Remember the tarot? The past is strangling the present? That's what happened to her—the past won't let go of her. Sneer all you want at psychic trauma, but you can't seriously believe she can be in love with the man who ruined her childhood and can have sex with him without doing herself harm."

Fry shook his head. "You got it wrong. Sex wasn't my idea. I hate to kiss and tell, but she was the one who made the first move."

"And you went along with it ignoring everything you knew about her. Didn't it ever occur to you that she might be trying to screw herself beyond recognition and that you were helping her?"

"Look, if you want to luxuriate in the notion that she's some poor emotional wreck, then do so, but leave me out of it. She's attracted to me and I'm attracted to her. This is *now* we're talking about. She's an adult. No one is using anyone. No one is harming anyone."

My anger left me as quickly as it had come, and a chill spread through me. "It's not that easy," I said.

"Of course it isn't. Of course there is more to it than that. She affects me. Not the way she did as . . . years ago."

"As a little kid—that's what you can't get yourself to say. As a little kid you went down on."

He continued as if I hadn't said anything. "I care about her. She matters to me. That's why I didn't want her to get hurt. That's why I didn't want her to drive that damn car again."

"I thought the motto is: Everything a man has will he give for his life."

Fry shook his head. He looked tired. "Not everything." His voice dropped and he seemed to be talking to himself. "Not while the sun is out. Not while he isn't wrapped head to heel in black terror." He pulled himself up as if making a final effort and looked at me directly. "I know you won't believe me, but whatever vision you have of me as a monster ensnaring a defenseless creature, then or now, is wrong. At any rate, what happened then happened. It's over."

"Nothing is that simple. You don't do certain things in your life without paying for them."

He let out a short laugh. "You and the Bible," he said. He checked his watch. "You'll have to excuse me. I have a doctor's appointment five minutes ago. Nothing that a few red pills won't do wonders for." He rose, took out his wallet and put several bills on the table and weighted them down with the sugar bowl.

"Where's Vida?" I asked.

"At the Institute, at the library. Second building on the right, second floor. I assume you feel you have to tell her everything and save her from my evil scheme."

"We're leaving today."

"Which proves, I suppose, that you believe in my coincidence theory. I'm flattered."

"I don't know what I believe."

"Believe in what you want to believe in and it may come true."

"Correlation by likeness."

"Precisely. Goodbye, John. I wish you well." Fry walked across the piazza, to where the Mercedes was parked. He drove off after giving me a wave.

I sat, wrapped in thought, replaying the conversation, trying to make sense of the pieces. At the periphery of my thinking lurked an uneasiness. I had the compelling feeling that I was forgetting something of vital importance and great urgency, something I needed to act on this instant. Then my mind made the connection: a tarot card appeared before me—the tower shattered by lightning—and I knew what I had forgotten. I got to my feet and began to run, along the piazza, down the road, then two steps at a time down the long stairway.

The door to the apartment was unlocked but Jim was gone. After a frantic search I found the keys to the Fiat and raced to the Institute. I worried that the guards would insist on someone to vouch for me, but when I told them in

English that I needed to see my wife, one of them shrugged, said something in Italian and waved me through. I drove on to the library, where Vida, surrounded by books, did not look at all pleased to see me. I spurted out that I couldn't explain now but I knew Jim was in danger and I had to drive to the duke's tower. I told her to go to the villa at once, lock the door and let in no one but me or Jim. When she didn't jump up to follow my instructions but looked at me as if I had lost my mind, I said, "I think Fry is trying to kill Jim." When that produced an even more pronounced reaction of incredulity, I added, "I know who Fry is. I know that you knew him years ago. And he knows it, too: he recognized you."

Her face went blank but she stood up, grabbed her parka and said, "I'm coming with you."

On the way to the tower I told her hurriedly and disjoint-edly about everything that had happened, everything I knew, leaving out only that Jim had known her when she was a child. Although I was close to incoherent, she asked no questions and only gave me instructions on where to turn.

We reached the dirt road. The Mercedes was parked in the grove at the end of the road. We ran through the trees, Vida pulling ahead of me. Then she stopped and I collided with her.

In the light of a gray day, the tower looked even more massive than I remembered it. Its door was wide open. Next to it Jim sat, his back against the wall. A few feet from him lay Fry, dead. Fry was lying on his back very straight. With the exception of a dark stain under the back of his head, the only sign of injury was one of his hands bent an impossible angle with respect to his arm. From that limp hand I got the terri-fying impression that his body could have been twisted into any configuration. His eyes were half closed, as if he were listening to something. I wondered whether I ought to close them, but I thought of the darkness he had described to me and was afraid I would in some way deprive him of light if I did.

A small sound came from Vida's throat and she walked up to the body and knelt down next to it.

I asked Jim, "Are you all right?"

He rose to his feet. "He tried to kill me," he said, looking at Fry. "He came to the villa—he had a key and a gun—and he made me drive the car here. He made me climb to the top of the tower—he said I'm the *sagitta*, and the *sagitta* is the tower in the old tarot. He told me to sit on the railing like Vida and I did that night. I think he was hoping for some crazy coincidence to happen. He knew I was in love with Vida. Maybe that made me like the unhappy lover of the legend. Maybe I was supposed to discover that I couldn't live without her and to throw myself off. I just sat there, waiting for him to flip out completely and put a bullet in my back. But instead he gave me a shove—that's what I call giving coincidence a hand. I managed to grab the railing, and I grabbed him with my other hand and he went over the edge."

Vida had listened without once taking her eyes off the dead man. Without looking up, she said, "You didn't have to kill him."

Jim stood, his feet squarely planted, his hands in the pockets of his bomber jacket, looking down on her. "No, you're right. I could have let him kill me. That could be me lying there. Except if it were, you wouldn't be kneeling beside me." He explained to me: "I wouldn't be that important. After all, I didn't molest her when she was a kid—you have to do something pretty spectacular before she starts giving a damn about you. You know what he said? He said he'd had a 'relationship' with her. That's a marvelous way of putting it, isn't it—'relationship'?"

"I know. He told me too."

"Am I surprised? I said to him, 'So you're the creep who screwed her up for life.'"

Vida began shaking her head with a dogged precision as if she didn't want anything to enter her ears.

Jim continued in a quiet fury, "And you know what the bastard said? He said, 'Is there anyone to whom she hasn't told the sad story of our star-crossed love?' That's when I thought of driving the car into the nearest tree. But I couldn't be sure he'd be dead.—He would have killed you, you know that?" he said to Vida. "You or John or me—it wouldn't have mattered which of us croaked, just so long as it wasn't him. So you can stop tearing your hair out over him. Look at it on the bright side. If he'd killed me you'd have been stuck visiting him in jail the rest of his life."

Vida kept shaking her head until he stopped talking. Then she reached out and touched the dead man's lower arm, not the one with the broken wrist, and tugged at it. She started to cry silently, and I thought, Oh Lord, I don't know her at all. I said to Jim, "He knew he wouldn't get away with it. I suppose he would have grasped at anything. He was drowning, or felt he was."

Jim ignored me and kept looking at Vida, his shoulders hunched in anger. "Such grief," he said. "So much feeling for poor Geoff and nothing for anybody else. I tell you what. I'm glad I killed the bastard. I didn't have to, you know. He dropped the gun when I grabbed him. I could have just held on to him and climbed back. But I didn't. Remember his fucking tarot cards telling everybody about vital choices that had to be made. I made that choice when I yanked him off the top. I pulled as hard as I could, and I'm glad I did."

Vida was still tugging on the body's forearm, distractedly now, as if she had forgotten what she was doing.

Jim shook his head. "This is too crazy. I don't have to stick around for this." He turned and walked off toward the dirt road and was gone among the trees.

I said to Vida, "We have to tell somebody. The police, or somebody at the Institute. Let's drive back to town."

She didn't respond.

I touched her shoulder. "I know it hurts," I said.

She shrugged off my hand with a violent twitch. Her eyes remained on Fry's face.

"There's no point," I told her. "He's gone. And I don't believe he's at that place he was afraid of."

She looked up at me, daggers in her eyes. "Go away. You know nothing about him. Go away and leave me alone."

"I know he cared about you. As much as someone like he could care about anybody."

Pronouncing each word with a quiet fury, she said, "Leave me alone."

I went to the car and waited. Some ten minutes later she appeared, saying calmly, "I don't want you here. Go back to the villa. I'll be there in a while. I won't do anything crazy, if that's what you're afraid of. I won't leap off the tower, and I won't drive the car into a tree."

She returned to the tower, and I walked down the dirt road and hiked along the country road toward town. A few kilometers later a couple with their teenage son stopped for me and offered me a ride. Pleased to discover an opportunity to practice their English, they involved me in a conversation about the difference between the American and Italian school systems. Answering their questions, I felt I had suddenly been propelled into a comedy of the absurd. On one part of the stage was my wife, heartbroken over the death of the man she'd been in love with, on another part was I, saying: "In junior high school the students move from room to room for different classes." They left me off near the villa, the third part of the stage, convinced they had had an edifying conversation.

Jim was in the living room putting things in his carryon bag. He greeted me with a grin that was a grimace and returned to packing. He looked like he'd been crying. I was dead-tired, and I sat down on the couch and said everything would be all right. Vida would recover; she'd already seemed better when I'd left her at the tower. Nobody was to blame. "Blame Fry's demented coincidences," I said.

"You don't believe that yourself," he said. "That everything will be all right. I've been thinking: You know why she wanted us to come along to Italy? Because she wanted me to come along, and she couldn't take me without taking you. She wanted her revenge on Fry, that's what it was all about. And she brought me to do the job for her. She knew how I felt about her and she knew how furious I was when she told me about Bliss the child molester. Maybe if she told me in just the right way, at just the right time, that here was the man who'd done this terrible thing to her, I'd go berserk and break his neck. She didn't have the guts to do it herself—a real chip off the old block—but what a great solution that would be. Talk about irony: now that I've done the job for her, she's in mourning over him."

The low hum of the gate made him stop. We looked at the door when Vida walked in. She cast a vague look in our direction as she swept through the living room, and she firmly closed behind her the door to the corridor. Jim's anger had left him. He looked at me imploringly and moved to follow her. I said, "She'll be all right in a while. Just leave her be." His mouth moved and he swallowed hard. He seemed on the verge of following Vida anyway but turned and went back to rummaging in his bag.

The door opened and suddenly Vida was in the middle of the living room, one hand gripping the spear gun's shaft, the other around its pistol grip. The triangular tip of the protruding spear was sharp, and corrosion on it looked like old blood. I had a mental impression of an arrow hissing through the air and striking a tree with a high ring. Jim turned. The gun was pointed at his chest. Then I was on my feet, between him and Vida.

She shouted, "Get out of the way!"

I said, "It wasn't his fault. Don't!" and took a step toward her, reaching for the gun.

There was a twang and a tearing hurt in my chest. I tried to breathe but couldn't. I thought, Fry was right, everything is connected. I was afraid of blacking out and falling forward, driving the shaft I was fingering further in. But Jim clamped his arms around me from the back and lowered me to the floor in the darkness crowding me.

I regained consciousness hours after the operation, and it took days before I found out what had happened after my "*accidente orribile*." Vida and Jim had gotten me to the hospital before I had died of respiratory failure. The surgery had been successful.

Jim left Italy for unknown parts almost the moment I came out of surgery with a favorable prognosis. Vida visited me daily at the hospital until I was transferred from Intensive Care to a semiprivate room. When I was able to walk up and down the hospital corridor, she told me that she was going back to the States. Not to New York though. She had met a couple who had lived for the past three years at a co-op in New Mexico, and they had invited her to spend a few months there.

No one knew of our presence at the tower when Fry had died. Vida told the police she'd seen him briefly in the morning and he'd seemed fine. His death was ruled suicide—a shock but no great surprise to people once they thought about it: Suddenly everyone knew that Fry had been in a morbid frame of mind for some time. Clear evidence of that frame of mind was found in a letter propped up on his desk at home and a box next to it. The envelope read: "In the event of my death," and it contained the instruction to place the contents of the box inside his coffin.

I read about Fry's clever contraption while I was still in the hospital. It was described in a somewhat ghoulish article on the great man that I found in an American magazine. Fry had designed a cylindrical case about the size of a pillbox and had had it machined out of a platinum-iridium alloy. In its lid was sunk a sapphire watch crystal, and the lid was sealed to the case with a gold gasket. Inside, he had covered the back surface with a high-grade luminous paint, a radium compound mixed with phosphor, which he had bought from a supplier in Ireland. "A modern-day version of the eternal light," Fry called it in the letter. The journalist had done his homework and had found out that the radium isotope used in the paint had a half-life of 1620 years and that the glow it emitted would, by a conservative estimate, still be discernible after 10,000 years.

The writer of the article more than hinted that a man who wanted a light in his coffin was mad. My own interpretation was that Fry's eternal light was no more than his final attempt at controlling coincidence: a light in his coffin to generate, through correlation by affinity, a light in a place of darkness that terrified him.

After I finished the article, I composed a list of the coincidences that had been necessary for Fry's life to end the way it had ended. Vida coming across an article on him was one, and so was the fact that in the same journal had been an ad for grants in interdisciplinary studies. Jim running into us that afternoon while Vida and I were arguing was another, and so was his being offered a compelling reason, in the form of my mad attacker, for becoming acquainted with us. His story of having just broken up with a girlfriend and therefore looking for an apartment I discounted as a probable lie, but my list kept growing: Vida encountering an echo of her father in my incompetent teaching assistant and getting to know me as a result; Jim as a boy staying at an aunt's house when Vida was bicycling by on her way to and from her professor. Then there was the coincidence of two contradictory aims leading to our presence in Italy: Vida scheming to see Fry, possibly in order to have her revenge; Fry inviting her with the idea that her presence would somehow save him.

I put away my list knowing that it was far from complete but suddenly superstitiously afraid that in completing it I would do harm. I drifted off to sleep wondering whether run-of-the-mill cause and effect wasn't ultimately the same as Fry's exotic acausal force, differently packaged, and convinced, as one can be convinced only in a dream, that hidden in that question lay the secret of the universe.

When Vida told me she was leaving for New Mexico, her mind was made up, and I didn't try to talk her out of her plan. The last time she visited me at the hospital, she did ask me, almost out the door, whether I'd be all right. I said, yes, I'd be fine. She'd hardly referred to Fry since his death, and I wondered whether she would now. But she left without mentioning him.

A month later I was on my way to New York. There I found a letter from Vida telling me she had discovered an unsuspected talent for pottery, the main source of income of the Double L Ranch co-op. The people there had told her they had never seen anyone progress as rapidly as she, and she had decided to extend her stay indefinitely. She asked me to send her a few things, mostly outdoor equipment, and to throw away anything else that was in my way. I sent her the requested items and did not throw away anything.

Jim was next: a few months after my return to New York, I received a photo glued to a postcard mailed in the Australian outback. In the photo, Jim, mugging the camera, was shearing a sheep. The card was addressed to Vida and me, and it read: "Having a wonderful time. Wish you were here." There was no return address.

Some months later I finished my book, and almost a year after that I found a publisher for it. I heard from Vida twice in eighteen months. One letter described a spectacular thunderstorm: the desert ablaze in sheet lightning, thunder roaring, a deluge pouring from the sky; the other contained an article about Double L pottery: the pieces that came out of the studio were becoming nationally recognized for their melding of traditional Indian motifs with a striking modernism. A picture of three pots had an arrow pointed at one—displaying a flamboyant pattern of light and dark geometrical shapes—and the legend: "Mine." In the letter, Vida wrote, "I'm proud how that one turned out. Of course it loses something in black and white."

I sat down on the spot to compose a reply, a virtual replica of the last letter I had sent her, telling her that I missed her, hated being without her, hoped to see her soon. Halfway through it, I balled it up and threw it in the wastepaper basket. The next day, I took a plane to New Mexico.

I rented a car at the airport and drove down an endless, unveering highway, a blue glass sky overhead, toward the mirage of an ever-receding patch of wet asphalt. At an intersection with a dirt road, a wooden sign directed me to the Double L Ranch. The sign had several bullet holes, one accidentally or deliberately dotting the L and turning it into a peculiar I. The ranch was a sprawling hacienda. A van and a pickup as well as several four-wheel drive rigs were parked in front. When I got out of the air-conditioned car, the heat felt like an enormous pressure from above. A Stetson-wearing boy no older than fourteen came out of the house, said hi, and got into the pickup. I went over to him and asked whether Vida was "around." He said, yes, she was getting some pieces ready for firing. "Just walk in," he said and drove off.

I walked into a hallway, cool and dark, and following the sound of voices found a kitchen, where a woman was fixing lunch and another, in a carpenter's apron, was installing shelving. Again I was greeted without curiosity, but was given directions to the kilns. There, surrounded by pots and plates on shelves and tables, was Vida in faded jeans and a belted turquoise tunic. She was painting an intricate design on a pot with what I assumed were glazes—pools of dark glassy colors in small ceramic containers.

She looked up, was surprised, said, "Why didn't you call?" and we conducted a perfectly inane conversation about my flight, and car rental, and at what time I had left New York, and how she could have picked me up at the airport if I'd called.

I asked her how she was, and she told me, fine, showed me the pot she was working on and explained some of the fine points of firing pottery. She also briefed me about the other members of the co-op: the boy I had met was somebody's son, the two women in the kitchen were photographers, altogether eleven people lived at the ranch. She asked me how I was, and it turned out that I, too, was fine; working on my second book, about a friend of my great-uncle who had founded a renegade political party in the thirties. I was digging up all sorts of interesting things.

I could see us chatting till doomsday about things having nothing whatsoever to do with the reason for my visit until somebody would show up and ruin any chance of a serious talk, but Vida finally asked, "Why did you come?" She looked at me directly, sending a shiver of gladness and fear through me.

"Because I want us to be together again," I said. "I don't care whether you come to New York or I move out here."

"Why?" Vida asked.

Of all the imaginary scenarios of our encounter I had constructed in the plane and during the drive, none had had this reaction from her. "Because I love you," I said.

"How can you if you don't even know me?" she said. "You don't, you know? You never knew a thing about me."

"How could I have. I was always on the outside and you kept the doors locked and the curtains drawn. Not that I helped things. I can't honestly claim that I tried to get in."

"Then how can you say you love me?"

"Because I do."

The thought came to me that this was the last time she ould allow me to talk to her openly. If I didn't succeed, she'd make an effort to avoid me or always be with other people in the future.

"There is nothing more tedious than one-sided attachments," I said. "But I know there was a time when you cared about me. All right, I disappointed you. I wasn't there when you needed me. I didn't want to know how much you needed me because I was afraid I wouldn't be able to help you, or because I was afraid I'd ruin everything if I knew. Or maybe

I just wanted everything to stay the same. But why can't we try again?"

"It's too late," Vida said.

I felt an awful fear. "Is there somebody else?" I asked, thinking I was reciting a rehearsed line.

"No, it isn't that."

"Then what is it?"

She shook her head angrily, her mouth tightly closed, as if that mute shake of the head would be the only reply I'd get. But then she relented: "How do you think I'd feel if I saw you with your shirt off?" she said, and when I looked startled, she added, "You see? You still don't understand. There's a scar, isn't there? Where the spear went in. It hurt you so badly. I hurt you. You couldn't breathe. You were gasping for air. I thought you were drowning in your own blood. And you were pulling on the shaft, like you were trying to get it out."

"I wasn't," I interrupted her. "I know I wasn't."

She wasn't listening to me. "I thought you were going to tear your lung out." She was crying. "You were hurt so badly. You looked at me. I knew you were asking me to help you and I didn't know how. Every time you'd take off your shirt, I'd see you again like that, with your fingers around that spear, asking me to help you. I couldn't stand it."

I didn't know how, but the space between us was gone. I was holding her. She kept sobbing. "It's all right," I said. "I'm fine. Better than before. The scar's an improvement." I patted her back, talked into her ear, told her that she hadn't meant to hurt me, that I never thought of that moment at all—not because it was painful to think about it but because it wasn't important, she was the only thing that was important to me. All the while I was so grateful to have her in my arms, even if just for a moment. She was holding on to me tightly, cling-ing to me. "Honestly," I said. "There's nothing to it. It's almost invisible."

I had a dazzling thought. "Here, let go," I said into her ear, backed her away and pulled my shirt and undershirt out of my pants. She didn't want to look, but then she did, at the thin pink scar marking the surgeon's incision, and the small triangular one at its center.

"Does it still hurt?" she asked.

"A twinge when the weather is about to change. More useful than any satellite forecast," I told her.

She let out a wet laugh, found a paper towel on one of the benches and blew her nose. "You're nice," she said. "At least I don't kill nice people."

"You haven't killed anyone. Even if you had, you meant no harm."

"I did mean Jim harm."

"Did you?"

"I must have. I tried to kill him, didn't I?"

"With an arrow, which is his name, which translates to *la sagitta*, which became The Tower—where Geoff died."

She looked puzzled.

"Correlation by affinity. The universe favoring coinci-dence."

"That's a cheap way out. The next thing you know nobody is to blame for anything—it's all coincidence, fate, whatever. It's not that easy." She paused, then said, "You should know this—I loved Geoff. I shouldn't have after what he did to my father and to me, but I did. I thought I hated him. When I read about him in that article I hated him so much that I wanted him dead. I thought I could somehow injure him by writing a book about him. Or maybe I thought I'd somehow make him die if I saw him again. Maybe there'd be some way—an accident I'd cause—something. But instead . . ." Her eyes suddenly brimmed again. "I loved him, I really did. Just as much as I did when I was twelve. I know it makes no sense. I know it's a sign of how screwed up I was. And still am. You know what I just thought? I thought, Why didn't he tell me he knew who I was? If he'd told me, we could have talked about what happened back then, and if we'd done that, maybe things would have worked out. And I don't even know what I mean by 'things working out.'"

She started crying earnestly again, and I took her into my arms and listened to her forlorn sobs and tried not to be hurt by my own interpretation of what "things working out" meant to her whether she knew it or not: Fry would not have died and they would have been happy together.

After a while she stopped crying. "I don't know," she said, still in my arms. "I really don't know if we could make it work after all this."

I rubbed her back. "Look at it on the bright side. It wasn't working fabulously well before all this."

She laughed. "You *are* nice."

I held her. "What happened between you and Geoff when you were a child?" I asked.

She moved away from me and looked at me with red eyes. "I thought Jim told you."

"I'd like you to tell me. And I'd like you to tell me what happened on the day your father killed himself. Will you tell me?"

"Maybe."

Hope lifted me up, but she quickly added, "I can't do it now."

"Why not now?"

"Because I have to know first if we'll be together. I don't know if we will."

"When will you know? How will you know?"

"I'm not sure. It'll take time. It's odd, but in all the time I've been here I've hardly thought about Italy. I need to do that. On my own."

"I can come back in a week. Or in two weeks."

"I don't know how long it'll take. I'll call you and tell you when I've decided."

I didn't try to talk her out of her resolution. After lunch with her and four or five of the other members of the co-op, I drove back to the airport and took a plane to New York.

And here I wait, one month and seventeen days after waving goodbye to Vida before driving away from the hacienda in a plume of sand.

My thinking these days is hopeful. I see the past as a dream behind us and the future as a dark land ahead. Fry passed on to me his fear of death, a three-in-the-morning dread of cold sweat and flesh shivering at the thought of its certain dissolution. But at all other times I'm cautiously optimistic or even cheerful, and I can attribute that to Fry as well. For with less distrust than he—with more amazement and hope—I recognize that patterns abound. The web is forever being woven, and the same hand that once before fused the thread of my existence with that of my Vida—my life—may do so again and may reunite me with Vida, short for Davida—which in our whimsical cosmos means "beloved."